FINDING GRACE

MAJOR MITCHELL

shalakopress.com

FINDING GRACE

For information contact: Shalako Press
http://www.shalakopress.com

ISBN: 978-1-7351297-6-1

Cover design: Karen Borrelli
Editor: Judith Mitchell

PRINTED IN THE UNITED STATES OF AMERICA

Acknowledgements

A big thank you to Judy for her editing.
She always turns my writing into something
legible.

Thank you to Karen Borrelli for her beautiful
cover art.

Most of all, thank you, the reader. You
are the ones who keep us crazy writers writing.

Dedication

This book is dedicated to *Without Permission* in Modesto, California, an organization actively saving young girls and boys from being kidnapped and becoming slaves.

ALSO BY THIS AUTHOR

The Valley of Decision

Poverty Flat

A Reason to Believe

Canyon Wind

The Doña Series
The Doña
Mokelumne Gold

The Manhunter Series
Manhunter
Where the Green Grass Grows

The Dusty Boots Series
Dusty Boots
Joker's Play
Refugio's Gold
Cool Water Justice

Children's Books
The Witch on Oak Street
Charlie Shepherd
I'm Molly

FINDING GRACE

Chapter 1

"The diner was built about thirty years ago by the current owner's father."

"Is the food any good?"

"You know, I've never eaten there. I do see a number of pickups and cars there every now and then." Jack did a nervous foot shuffle.

"The rest of the buildings popped up shortly thereafter. And no one knows how it got the name of Jackass Springs."

"How many people live here?" Cody asked as he scanned the greasewood and mesquite bushes dotting the area. The property had been on the market for what seemed an eternity with no one showing interest.

"There's around fifty, if you count the people living in campers out past the row of bushes over there." He pointed, and then quickly changed the subject.

"And, you'll never guess what's behind this panel," Jack said as he rolled the panel to the left. Even though the stainless-steel door was dusty and caked with cobwebs, Cody Waters knew exactly what it was. He had spent months scouring real estate ads and doing internet searches looking for a bomb shelter that was remote and out of the way. The only question in his mind was how large was the shelter behind the door.

"Now, why in the world would a man want to build a bomb shelter way out in the middle of the Mohave Desert?"

"Ah, you knew," Jack said with a laugh. "Who told you?"

"No one told me," Cody said and helped Jack pull the door open. "I used to build these things, years ago." He flipped the light switch but the lights failed to work.

"Huh, the batteries must be dead," Jack said as he tried the switch at the bottom of the stairs. "I'll see if I can't find someone to check them out."

"That might be good." Cody lit the flashlight mode on his cell phone and glanced around the interior quickly before returning to the stairs. He didn't bother to tell the realtor that the bomb shelter was a predecessor to the Extreme Patriot Bunker. He had worked on several of them, but this one was old, probably from the late seventies or early eighties, and from the decaying paper grocery sacks on the counter, it didn't look as though it had been used.

"I think the original owner may have built it because of Edwards Air Force Base."

"Maybe, but most sane people locate where the base isn't. It's a lot cheaper that way." He shaded his eyes against the sun as he turned in a slow circle.

"Okay," Cody heaved a sigh, "what are we looking at?"

"I beg your pardon?"

"I want to buy the lot. I own a towing company, and this is a perfect location." Cody walked toward the center of the property as he talked. "Right off Highway 14 halfway from Mohave to Lancaster. I've checked and there are a lot of people who break down or get flats on that piece of road. So, how much."

"Well, Cody Waters," Jack said with a smile, "let's go back to my office and talk numbers and see if we can make you an offer you can't refuse."

Several hours later Cody Waters climbed into the cab of his truck and started the engine. He pulled his cell phone from his pocket and dialed a number. "Yeah, I got it. We're in business. No, it needs some work. I can't tell you that

2

until I get the lights to come on. It gets kind of dark inside one of those. Yeah, I'll let you know."

Chapter 2

Six months later.

"Yes!" Grace Peterson shouted and pumped her fist in the air. She had spent the past two years skipping meals and missing sleep, juggling her time between school and spending time with her son.

"I take it you passed," Kirk Randall said with a chuckle. This wasn't the Grace Peterson he had just spent the last semester sitting beside in class. That Grace Peterson was reserved and seldom spoke. This woman had just earned a bachelor's degree in education, and a teaching credential. She deserved to celebrate.

"I aced it!" She pointed toward her name on the list the secretary had just loaded into the website.

Kirk grabbed her in a bear hug. "I knew you would. Let's go somewhere we can find decent food. How about Red Lobster? I'll buy."

"Oh, Kirk, I can't."

"Why not? Everyone has to eat. Even Jesus ate dinner with his disciples."

"I've been away from Matthew for four days now, and he's probably driving my mom insane. Besides," she slipped her arms around his neck and grinned, "knowing my mother, she probably has dinner started and wants to celebrate as a family."

"Yeah, but I happen to love you too. How am I supposed to compete with a two-year-old?"

"Oh, don't be jealous of my son. If you married me, you'd be marrying him too. You know that, don't you?"

"Yes, I do know that, but I can pitch a little fit of my own, can't I?"

They walked hand-in-hand toward the parking lot and stopped beside her blue Honda. The wind had started kicking up and clouds of dust were billowing on the horizon. Grace unlocked the car door and gave Kirk a quick kiss on the lips.

"I'll call you in a few days and let you know when you can visit the competition, if you want."

"Are you kidding? I've been begging to meet your son and your mother since I met you."

"Now you'll get your chance. I've got to go."

She kissed him again and ducked inside her car. Kirk Randall watched her pull away with a dark feeling inside his chest.

******

"Agh! No, not again." Grace yelled and pounded the steering wheel with her fists. The traffic had ground to a complete stop. Some people were exiting their cars in hope of seeing what lay ahead. One poor soul had taken off hiking but turned around and ran back to his car the instant the gusting wind peppered the side of her car with sand and bits of gravel.

Grace checked the instruments on her dashboard. She had plenty of gasoline and the oil looked fine. The coolant however seemed low and the temperature of the engine kept climbing higher. She looked around as if to find an answer hanging in the dusty air. She heaved a deep sigh and called her mother and told her about the dead traffic and that she had no idea when she'd arrive home. Her mother calmly looked at the traffic report on the internet.

5

"I hate to tell you this, honey, but there's been a major accident. A big rig overturned about five miles ahead of you and is completely blocking the highway, both ways."

"Well, my car's starting to overheat and I don't know what to do."

"Is there any place to pull over and turn the motor off?"

"Well, across the other lane. I see an old café and garage. I guess I could try there."

"Do that honey, and we'll celebrate tomorrow."

Grace cranked her steering wheel hard left, crept across the other lane and pulled into a large gravel parking lot then parked in front of the café. The interior lights were on and the word *EARL'S* painted on the window stood out clearly. She locked the car door and dashed toward the café. Besides the young man in the kitchen and a chunky waitress, there were only two customers inside the place.

"Whew," Grace said as she pushed her hair back with her fingers. "It is really windy out there."

"Yes, darlin' it is that. And according to the internet, it ain't supposed to stop until sometime tomorrow," the waitress said. "Besides a place to escape the wind, what can I get for you?"

"How about an ice tea with no sugar?"

"One sugarless tea coming up. It's a little early yet, but if you're hungry, Earl grills up a pretty good burger. You might want to try one."

She slid a tall tumbler of tea in front of Grace and smiled.

"By the way, my name's Sue."

"Well Sue, give me a few minutes to collect my thoughts and I might take a cheese burger. But first, my car was starting to heat up. Is there anyone around here that can take a look at it?"

"You might try Cody Waters over at the towing place." Sue pointed toward the barn. "I've had him tinker on my old clunker a couple of times and he seemed okay."

"Okay." Grace set the tea on the counter. "I'm going to take my car over there and be back as quick as I can. Then, I'll try the cheese burger."

Cody had her pull the Honda inside the barn and he lifted the hood. He plugged a computer into the car only to unplug it a few minutes later. He tinkered under the hood some more before pointing toward a spot on the engine.

"Looks like you need a new thermostat. See? You go on driving it like that and you'll ruin the engine."

"How do I get one of those? I'm kind of stuck here."

"Well, let me see." Cody rummaged through his meager collection of parts and returned with a small box.

"This here should take care of the problem. All we got to do is wait until the engine cools and I'll pop it in and you'll be on your way. That is, as soon as the traffic starts moving again."

"Yeah, there's always that. How come you're not out towing that big rig off the road?"

"The wreck is closer to Mohave than here. The Highway Patrol is using one of the wreckers in town."

"Do you take credit cards?"

"Yes I do. We can take care of it when you get back."

Grace returned to the café and ate half of her cheese burger and fries, then had Sue wrap the rest into a paper sack. The traffic was starting to creep like a snail and she wanted to check on the status of her car. She stopped at the door and stared as Cody Waters ran a damp towel across the hood of her car.

"Take a seat, ma'am. I'll be finished in a minute."

"Is it fixed?"

"Oh yes. Replacing a thermostat is real easy. It runs like a champ. Here," he pulled a chair to a small desk and cleared a space and sat her tea in the middle. "I just figured a nice car like this should look as good as it runs."

"Thank you. It's starting to get old, but it really is a good car."

She sat sipping her tea as Cody finished drying the car. She yawned several times as he hung the towel and went to fetch his card scanner. As she watched him slide the card her head rolled to one side and she fell from the stool.

Chapter 3

"Where am I?"

Grace sat up too quickly and had to grab her head.

"Headache?"

"King-sized. Where am I," she repeated.

"You're in my special place," Cody said as she looked around. "You don't have to worry. There's only a couple of people who even know this place exists. Would you like some coffee? I make good coffee."

"No, I want to go home and see my mother and my son. He's only two years old and needs his mother."

"Well, that's the problem now."

"What's a problem?"

"I'm not sure I can just let you walk out of here just yet."

"Why not? Why can't you let me walk out of here?"

"I can't let you do that because you know who I am and where I live. You'll just go to the police or the sheriff's department and tell them a bunch of lies and they'll haul me off to jail."

"Now, why would I do that, Cody? I just barely know who you are. Besides, what is it that you've supposedly done? You gave me a bed to sleep in when we were having a nasty dust storm. Now, I just want to go home."

"W-e-l-l," he drug the word out as he gazed over her long brown hair and blue eyes. She looked as though she

9

had been created by a master. "You came in here last night and you were the prettiest woman I'd ever seen. I just needed to talk to you. I wanted to see if it was possible for someone like you to like someone like me."

"What are you saying, Cody?" She got out of bed and poured herself a mug of coffee. "If you wanted to talk, all you had to do was say so. I would have talked to you. But now," she shrugged, "I need to go home."

She felt a cold chill creep up her spine as Cody began shaking his head.

"No, I've been trying to tell you. I have some business partners who would get mad. I can't let you do that. You have to stay here with me."

Chapter 4

Chase woke with a headache and a scowl on his face, but that didn't stop his sister from shaking him.

"Wake up. You've got company."

"Go away!" He pulled the pillow over his face, trying to will her into the barn. "I didn't get home until one-thirty, and I need some sleep."

"Get up! She's a cash-paying client, and you haven't had too many of those the past couple of months. You need the money." She shook him again. "The ranch could use your rent money."

Chase removed the pillow to glare at her. "You're not going away, are you?"

"Not until I'm sure you're getting up." She dropped to the mattress and bounced several times.

"Okay, okay, okay," Chase raised his hands. "I'm getting up. You'd think my rent would afford me a little privacy and sleep."

Janice stopped with her hand on the door handle to give him a crooked grin.

"May I remind you, Chase McGraw, that you're two months behind on the cheapest rent in Bakersfield. That affords you access to the entire ranch, but you don't get to snub new clients. Now, get dressed and come into the office, or I'll bring her in here to see you. I've got coffee and cinnamon rolls waiting."

She closed the bedroom door and he tossed back the comforter while he mentally compared Janice Adams to a blood-sucking insect. He loved his sister, but on the other

11

hand, Janice could be like a horse fly that kept returning for another bite, no matter how many times you swatted at it.

"She hasn't changed a bit from when we were kids," he said, slipping into a pair of jeans and his brown cowboy boots. They had played together as kids for hours without many squabbles. She would play the part of a bank robber or some other evil villain, just as long as he'd play house with her next. He didn't mind it too much, except when she asked him to give the doll a bath and change its diaper.

He brushed his teeth and splashed cold water on his face. He and Janice had been the only children their parents had, and since they lived on this ranch, they soon became best friends. He had stood at her wedding when she married Bob. Bob Adams, in Chase's opinion, was the only guy worthy of Janice. Then, six years later he'd stood with her again when Bob died of leukemia. That was when she inherited this ranch, which was proving to be a blessing and a curse at the same time. She in turn had stood at his side when his wife, Rita, asked for a divorce.

He stumbled down the hallway and stopped at an opened door. His office happened to be a desk and one file cabinet in the far corner of the ranch's business office. Janice was holding a cute little boy with frosting around his mouth, and talking to an attractive woman.

"There he is," Janice said with a snicker. "I told you he was alive."

"Hi," he said with an appraising nod as he plopped into the swivel chair behind the desk.

"Hello, I'm Marti Black. And the boy with the dirty face is Matthew, my grandson."

"Uh, please," Chase turned away. "Let me get a cup of coffee down first. I was in Los Angeles divorce court all day yesterday, and didn't get in until one-thirty in the morning.

"Right on the desk like I said," Janice said.

"Not your own divorce I hope." Marti said.

"No," Chase paused to take a sip. "Mine happened three years ago. This was for a client."

"Do you like horses?" Janice asked the boy and got a happy nod as he took another bite of cinnamon roll.

"Well, that's good. Come with me while those two talk business, and I'll show you Easy. He's my horse. We'll feed him an apple, and he might let you sit on his back." She took Matthew's hand and headed toward the door. "I also know where a momma cat has her kittens."

"You be good for Mrs. Adams, Matthew," Marti called after them.

"They'll be alright," Chase said, taking another sip of coffee. "Believe me. I've never seen anyone as good with kids as my sister. How old is he?"

"He's two. How many children does she have?"

"None. They didn't have any children when her husband died. Now she just pours out her love on everyone else's kids." He set the cup aside and studied her for a few seconds. "We don't get many clients to the ranch." *Certainly not as pretty as you.* "What can I do for you?"

"Find my daughter, Mr. McGraw." Marti reached into her over-sized handbag to retrieve a file folder. "This is everything the Sheriff's Department has on the case. She's been missing for several weeks…almost a month, and I'm sure something bad has happened to her."

Chase thumbed through the file, pausing a few seconds to study a photograph. "Looks like her mother."

"Yes, she does. Will you try to find her?"

"Who sent you to me?"

"A sheriff's deputy named Robert Thornton. Why?"

"No reason." Chase refilled his cup and grinned. "Usually, the sheriff's department and the city police don't want private investigators nosing around their cases. I was just wondering."

He took another sip and closed the folder.

13

"Don't worry." He chuckled at the expression on Marti's face. "Bob Thornton is a good man. If he asked you to look me up, I'm sure he has his reasons."

"So, you'll try to find her?"

"This is really close to becoming a cold case. They may not be calling it that, but anything this old will be difficult digging up information on. I would like to spend a day or so looking at the file, and then I'll get back to you."

"Okay." She tried to laugh but what came out sounded more like a sob. "I thought I'd feel better after talking to you, but I don't. You haven't given me much hope."

"I have a policy of telling clients exactly what they'll be facing. If I think I'll find your daughter, or discover what happened to her, I'll give you a hundred percent. But if I don't think there's much hope, I'll tell you that also."

"Do you have any idea what this might cost?" Several tears spilled over and trickled down her cheeks.

"Not until I get into it. The best I can do is guess."

He waited a minute while she fumbled for a tissue inside her purse.

"I charge $300 a day plus expenses. I've had several missing person cases that went rather quickly and several others that went nowhere." He shrugged. "That's the nature of this type of case."

"Alright, Mr. McGraw." She dabbed her eyes and forced a smile. "Here's my telephone number. I'll wait for your call." She handed him a slip of paper.

"And what about your husband? How does he feel about all this?"

"I don't have a husband." She rose rather quickly. "Mr. Black and I were divorced several years ago also. He knows Grace is missing, but that's the extent of it. He still hasn't bothered to call to find out about her. I have to find her myself."

"Okay." Chase got up and held the back door open. "Tell me about Grace. Maybe it'll help."

"Grace was always studious. A straight "A" student through high school and college. That was where she met Carl, her husband, in college. They got married right away. Then she dropped out when she got pregnant. Matthew, that little boy, is her son. Then Carl joined the Army and got killed in Iraq. It was quite a blow to Grace."

"I'm sorry to hear that. It must have been pretty tough on both of you." Chase led her out the rear of the house and toward the barn. Janice had the horse tied to the corral with Matthew sitting on his back.

"But after a period of grieving, Grace decided to return to college to get her bachelor's degree and teaching credential. Now, this."

"Well, I'll see what I can do," Chase said as they stopped at the corral.

"It's time to leave now, Matthew. See if Mrs. Adams will help you down," Marti said, and received a pouty whine.

"That's okay," Janice said as she lifted him off Easy. "You and your grandma can come back and ride horses anytime."

She had just set Matthew on the ground when a border collie rounded the barn and charged toward them with a loud bark. Marti caught her breath and lunged toward the boy but Chase caught her by the arm.

"That's Buster. He won't hurt him." The dog instantly started licking Matthew's sticky face, causing a fit of giggles to erupt from the boy.

"How was I supposed to know?"

"You wouldn't. Buster was top dog around here for years, but age has caught up with him. Now, he's enjoying retirement. Aren't you, old boy." Chase squatted and held the dog as Marti rescued her grandson.

"Well, thank you for your time, Mr. McGraw. It's been educational, to say the least." She offered him her hand. Chase smiled as he shook it. The cuff of what had been an expensive business suit was frayed.

"Come on, I'll walk you to your car." Chase held Matthew while she got his car seat ready. "I promise, I'll call you within two to three days."

"I'll wait to hear from you."

She closed the door of her Ford Escape and drove away. The car's dark blue paint was faded and the engine coughed a puff of smoke as she shifted gears.

"Well, what do you think?" Janice asked as she tossed a saddle blanket on Easy.

"Judging from her clothes and the condition of her car, I don't think she can afford a private eye."

Chapter 5

"No, what I gave her is everything we've got. I personally copied the entire file." Bob Thornton filled two mugs with coffee and passed one to Chase.

"It isn't very much," Chase said with a shrug.

"No, but it's what we've got. She arrived at college three weeks ago and took her test. Then, her friends at school and two professors all saw her kiss her boyfriend goodbye and climb back into her car and drive away. Then?" Bob shrugged, "she just disappears. Nada...zilch." Bob paused to take a sip of coffee and made a face.

"Not very good?" Chase asked.

"Tastes like it was made with motor oil. Come on," he set his mug on the counter and headed toward the door. "The hotdog stand out by the court house has better coffee. I'll treat. Sarah?" he paused at the receptionist's desk, "Chase and I are going for coffee. Do you want anything?"

"Sure, if you're buying."

"Yeah, I'll treat today."

"I'm not getting away for lunch so I'll take a Polish."

"One Polish sandwich with fries and coffee coming up," Bob said as he pushed through the door.

Chase followed him out the door and down one flight of stairs and then the street. He chuckled to himself as they paused for some traffic. He had automatically fallen back into the position he had held for ten years when he had worked for the department. Bob Thornton had been his supervisor back then, and they had become close friends. They had gone to each other's houses for barbeques and watched Bob's oldest son's baseball games. That all seemed to change when Rita filed for a divorce. To this day, she'd never said why. Her only excuse was she didn't want to be married to a cop. That didn't make much sense to Chase, since he was employed by the County Sheriff's Department when they started dating. That was when he started drinking.

Bob Thornton warned him about the drinking, and did his best to hide it from everyone else. He invited Chase to go to church with him and his family, but Chase was seething with anger at the time and attending church with Bob and his family was not very high on his list of things to do. That was the first time he remembered thinking of Bob Thornton and his family as being black.

The hammer fell the day County Sheriff James West heard Chase was intoxicated on the job, and called him into his office.

"I'm sorry, Chase. I've read your record and it's impeccable. I want you to join A.A., or some other group to get some help. If not...I'll have to let you go. I can't have one of my officers drunk on the job."

That was two years ago. Rita got her divorce and he got canned. He found out later that Rita had a boyfriend and figured that was why she wanted out. It was Janice who finally got him to quit drinking. She talked him into coming to the ranch, and then stole all the keys to the vehicles. She then trashed all the booze on the ranch and stayed by him until he had completely dried out. They even started going to church and both had become Christians. They were both baptized the same day.

******

"Three Polish sandwiches with everything, and three coffees," Bobby said to the short Mexican who ran the cart. He claimed his name was Juan Martinez, but Chase had been a deputy sheriff at the time he had applied for a business license and had run a background check on him. He discovered his real name was Juan Jesus Castro. He had made a living as a prize fighter and became rated as a middle-weight contender, until he got addicted to drugs. He asked Juan about it one time and received a shoulder shrug in answer.

"Here," Bobby handed Chase a sandwich wrapped in white paper and a Styrofoam cup of coffee. "Carry those and lead the way. I don't want to drop anything."

Chase took the lead, chanting, "Coming through" every now and then. He held the door open while Bobby delivered Sarah's order.

"You got three messages while you were gone." Sarah handed Bobby several slips of paper. Take care of Mayor Parker first. I told him you'd just stepped out and would call him in..." she checked her clock..."about fifteen minutes. The rest can wait until later."

"Thanks, Sarah. You're an angel," Bobby said.

"Yeah, tell that to my kids."

They sat at Bobby's desk and to eat their sandwiches.

"Come on now," Bobby said over a mouthful. "Don't you miss this place just a little?"

"Sure," Chase said with a nod. "I spent...what? Seven years in the uniform. What I really miss is a regular paycheck."

"Why don't you come back then? We've got a couple more rules, but nothing you can't handle. Besides, most of the guys know you."

"Yeah, and they all know I went kind of nuts and started drinking. Nah," he shook his head, "they'd all be wondering if I had their backs, and that's kind of important."

"You might be surprised." Bobby laid his sandwich aside and took a sip of coffee. "Anyway, back to this missing persons thing. What we do know is that Grace Peterson had gone to Phoenix to take a final college exam. I've seen the test results and she aced the test—straight A's. Then she climbed into her car and left Phoenix, supposedly to return to Bakersfield. We've got a half dozen people, including her boyfriend, who said they'd all stand up in a court and swear to it."

"That's something new," Chase said, wiping his mouth and fingers.

"What's new?"

"The boyfriend. This is the first I've heard of him. How close were they and where does he live?"

"He's listed in the file," Bobby said, shoving the last bite into his mouth. "They attended classes together. He works for the university, and I think he teaches computer science. According to him, they were close but not lovers. He's easy to find. I did interview him twice and he denies having anything to do with her disappearance and for some weird reason, I think he's telling the truth."

"You don't mind me interviewing him again, do you?"

"No, I expected you would. That's why I listed all his information for you. Now, if you'll excuse me, I need to call the mayor."

"Okay, that's my cue to leave. Thanks for the lunch."

"No problem."

Chase could hear Bobby's voice schmoozing Mayor Parker as he closed the door. He waved toward Sarah, who was also on the phone, as he passed her desk and bounced down the stairs and out into the street. He was feeling hopeful. He waited for the light to change then crossed the street with a small mob of pedestrians who had been waiting in the hot sun. He climbed into his truck and started the engine then cranked the air conditioner on full-blast, rolled down his windows and waited for some of the heat to escape. It had been a while since he'd worked on what he would call a real case.

Maybe Janice was right, he was losing his touch. He had been feeling stale and listless. Perhaps this was just what the doctor ordered—something to stir the juices and get him thinking.

Chapter 6

Chase drove to the nearest newspaper, The Bakersfield Californian, and asked to see anything concerning the date Grace had disappeared and shortly thereafter. The jackknifed big rig on Highway 15 that had caused a traffic backup of several miles was the headline article. It was followed by a weather-related story about the strong wind that swept the Mohave Desert causing dust storms, and a story about the war in the Mideast. Then there was something about a male coach of a girls' softball team being accused of sexual misconduct with a couple of players, but nothing about Grace Peterson. Grace didn't appear until the next day, after she'd been missing for twenty-four hours. *That's typical*, he thought.

After exhausting the archives of the Californian, Chase drove to the office of The Daily Report and asked to see their files. He found it pretty much the same as The Californian, and the Bakersfield News Observer again was almost identical to the other two. *That's what you get when you get your stories from an online news agency.*

He drove to the ranch and began laying out a chart on a whiteboard in order to see what had really taken place. Janice entered the office and peered over his shoulder silently for a few minutes pointing at the chart.

"Think the windstorm had anything to do with her disappearing?"

"I think it had something to do with it…maybe a little, but I don't know exactly how much. If she was alright and had just pulled over until the wind stopped, she would have driven home when the wind let up. She might've been late, or come in the next day, but she'd be home."

"So, where does that leave you?"

"Exactly where I've been since I told Marti I'd do my best." He chuckled and shook his head. "Grace Peterson left college after taking the final exam and disappeared. Poof!" He used his hands like a magician making something vanish. "The big problem is people don't just disappear. Even those who have something bad happen like being kidnapped eventually turn up, at least most of the time. I've got a feeling that *someone*, not *something*, caused Grace to disappear."

"So now what?"

"Tomorrow I start where Bob Thornton started by making telephone calls and interviewing witnesses." He shrugged. "You never know. Maybe someone remembers something that's not in the report."

"Well, good luck," she said, patting him on the shoulder. "Dinner's ready."

Chapter 7

Grace readied herself as she heard Cody's massive key ring rattle against the door. She had to give him credit for promptness. He always arrived at seven o'clock every evening with a dinner tray. The trouble was, the diet was extremely limited. Hamburgers and grilled cheese sandwiches with French fries or onion rings—most anything fried and greasy. She figured she'd gain twenty pounds sitting around inside the bomb shelter with nothing to do but eat.

Cody brought her text books and travel bag and purse to her the day following her abduction. Her driver's license and all her credit cards were in order. The little surge of thankfulness and compassion she had felt quickly melted into depression and anger. If he was willing to return her cards and license, that must mean he had no plans of her ever going free.

But things were going to be different tonight. The good Lord willing, she was going to burst out of her prison and escape. Her mother had to be going stark-raving mad worrying about her. They had always been close, but her mother had literally become a saint after Carl died. Thank God she had Matthew with her. Grace ached to hold her baby boy. She was determined that tonight would change things. It was all about freedom.

The door swung open and she sprinted like a track star coming out of the blocks. "Ahhh!" She caught a glimpse of surprise on Cody's face as she darted past and ducking out of his weak grasp as he fought to keep from spilling the contents of the tray. She charged up the stairs and threw herself against the door, but the steel door held fast. Glancing back over her shoulder, she could see Cody casually placing the tray on the table.

Grace grabbed the door handle and tried several more times but to no avail.

"Open, you stupid door. Open!" she screamed as Cody turned away from the table and walked casually toward her. She burst into tears and slowly slid to the floor.

"Please...please. Why won't you let me go home? Please!"

"I could have told you that wouldn't work." Cody stopped where she sat on the floor like a melted puddle of ice. "The doors will latch themselves, unless you prop them open. And, the only way to open them is with my keys. Anyway, it was a nice try. You run pretty darned fast for a girl."

He held out a hand to help her up.

"Come on. Let's eat dinner, and you can talk about anything you want. I promise."

Grace allowed him to lead her toward the table. She would allow Cody Waters to do most of the talking, since he seemed to like talking. If what he said was true, she would have to figure out a way of getting the keys away from him. That was another problem for her to pray about.

Chapter 8

The following day Chase stayed inside the office with his ear glued to the telephone, interviewing Grace's friends. Every one of them told the same story: Grace was a kind, loving and compassionate person who went out of her way to help others. Grace was hoping to become a teacher and would have made a great one. A couple of the girls broke down and cried while telling him what they knew. He felt like he was trying to find a young Mother Teresa by the time he'd finished.

Grace's boyfriend, Kirk Randall, was a different story. He was teaching a class on computer science and couldn't be reached. Chase left a message requesting a return call but as of four o'clock had not received one. He was about ready to call again when the phone rang.

"Hello."

"Hi, this is Kirk Randall. I'm returning a call from a Mr. Chase McGraw."

"I'm Chase. I've been hired to find out what happened to Grace Peterson. Would you mind answering a few questions for me?"

"Certainly not. Ask away."

"Would you mind if I record our conversation?"

"Not at all, go ahead."

"Thank you. I'm turning on the recorder now."

Chase turned on the recorder and grabbed a legal pad and pen. For the next 43 minutes he re-asked every question that Bob Thornton had asked then added several of his own. In the end, he found himself back where he was at the beginning. He tended to agree with Bob Thornton that Kirk Randall had nothing to do with Grace's disappearance. He placed the phone back into the cradle and laid his head against the desk.

"Rough day?"

He looked up to see his sister standing in the doorway.

"This one's almost got me wishing I hadn't quit drinking. What's up?"

"Walt and I are thinking of running into town for burgers and fries. Wanna come?"

"You kidding? Give me five minutes."

Chase splashed cold water in his face and made himself presentable, wondering about Walt Rogers. Walt was a professional team roper who had gotten hurt and had to take a year off to mend. Janice felt sorry for him and needed the extra help, so she hired him. They discovered Walt's knowledge about cattle and ranching made him a valuable asset to have around. But when the year came to an end, Walt just kept on working for his sister and bypassed another season. He'd asked Janice about him and got a shoulder shrug in return.

They ordered burgers, fries and Pepsi's then slid into a booth.

"So, your sister's been telling me about this case you're working on. Fill me in on some of the details," Walt said.

"Well, right now I'm feeling like I've entered some time warp or something. I have half a dozen people who witnessed her leaving school and driving away; then she's gone, including her car. No one's seen neither Grace nor her car."

Chase spent the next ten minutes telling Walt all he knew about Grace Peterson, pausing only to take a drink when their orders arrived.

"Huh," Walt said as he poured catsup on his fries. "I guess detecting isn't too different from rodeoing."

"How's that?" Janice asked over a bite of cheeseburger.

"Well, all the horses and bulls and their riders are supposed to be assigned by lottery to make it fair. But when you get to know the inside workings, there's a lot of swapping and horse trading going on inside the pens. I'll bet you a steak dinner that what happened to that girl has nothing to do with her friends or family."

"So what do you think happened to her?" Janice asked.

"I don't know that exactly. My guess is that somebody snatched her on the way home. But that's Chase's job."

"Well," Chase said wiping his lips with a napkin. "I'm beginning to think you might be right. I just have to figure out where the abduction took place, and if anyone saw it."

Chapter 9

Grace sat on the sofa watching, as Cody Waters entered the room with an armful of new magazines and a couple of movie CDs.

"I hope you like to read." He placed them in the center of the coffee table and grinned. "That was a stupid thing to say. Of course you like to read. You just finished college, didn't you?"

"Yes, I do like to read. Where's my Bible?"

"I beg your pardon?"

"I asked where my Bible was. I had it inside the car with me, but it's not with my things you brought in. I'd like to have it."

"Yes, I remember seeing it. Do you really read that thing?"

"Of course I read it. Why wouldn't I?"

"Well, I've never met anyone who liked to read the Bible like they was reading a regular book. Know what I mean?" Cody laughed and shuffled his feet.

"Well, I do. Can you get it for me?"

"Sure, I can get it for you. Give me a few minutes."

Grace leaned back on the sofa saying a silent prayer of thanks as Cody unlocked the door and ascended the staircase. She had no idea how long she had been without the word of God, but five minutes was too long, let alone several days. A few minutes later she heard the keys rattle. The door opened and he entered, carrying her Bible in his left hand.

"One Bible coming up," he said with a stupid grin. "I had it hidden under the driver's seat." He handed Grace the Bible and stepped back.

"Thank you so much." Grace could feel her eyes mist over as she took the Bible. "Now, I can catch up."

"Catch up on what?"

"Catch up on my Bible studies," Grace said with a small chuckle.

"You study that book for the fun of it?"

Grace stared at Cody for a minute before nodding slowly.

"Yes, I do, usually every morning, if you must know. It helps me get through the day."

"Okay, read me something." Cody had a smirk on his face. Grace said another silent prayer as she cleared her throat.

"Okay, what would you like to hear?

"I don't care. Just read something."

"Alright, this is from Luke, and it's about two men who went to the temple to pray."

It wasn't a story Grace would have chosen, but she read the parable slowly and clearly. When she had finished, Cody stood quietly staring at her for a few minutes.

"Who was telling the story you read?"

"That was Jesus telling that story."

"Huh," Cody began waving his arms and acting crazy as he talked. "Well, I can't believe that's true since there's no such a person as Jesus."

"You don't believe Jesus exists?" Grace was caught off guard and stuttered slightly.

"Oh, he exists alright, the same as the Easter Bunny or Santa Claus."

"Oh no, He's a real person. And He loves you."

Cody started laughing hysterically. "I used to believe in some of that back when I was a kid, but not anymore."

"Why, Cody? What happened to turn you away?"

"My mom raised me by herself because my old man decided to drink himself to death. There was this little church not too far from our house and my mom would get me up every Sunday morning and dress me in the best clothes I had and off to Sunday school we'd go. Teacher and the preacher always said things just like you read, but I must've been the only one inside the church that listened, because everyone else lived like the devil hisself."

"Oh, I'm so sorry…"

"I'm not done," Cody cut her off.

"The kids in the class I attended used to make fun of the way I was dressed, and a couple of times several of the bigger guys beat me up, and one time took away my pants. Later on, my mom discovered she had cancer. Not one person from that church called or came by to visit. She died all alone with just me to mourn her dying. And that's," he pointed at her, "why I don't believe Jesus exists."

"I am so sorry, Cody. I really am."

"Yeah, well don't feel too bad about it. I'm a big boy now, and I've gotten even a couple of times." He walked to the door and opened it.

"Oh, I forgot. I got a call from a business associate, and you'll probably have some company tomorrow night. Enjoy your Bible." He left, making sure the door was locked and secure.

When he was gone Grace knelt beside the sofa and quietly uttered a prayer for Cody Waters' soul.

Chapter 10

"Why?"

"Because I said so."

Marti stared at the little boy at her feet. She had dressed him that morning in a pair of bib coveralls with tennis shoes and a Cookie Monster hat. With his blond hair and crystal-blue eyes, he was cute enough to take a bite out of. He had been begging her to take him to see the horses at Janice's ranch, and she had been firm telling him no.

"Why?"

"Because Grandma has some things she really needs to do."

"Wanna Horsey," he whined and tugged on the leg of her faded Levi's.

"Yes, I know what you want, and I still say no."

"Why?"

"You're too young to understand. That horse belongs to Mrs. Adams, and you just can't go out to their ranch anytime you want to ride it."

"Why?" he said with a long whine and dropped to the floor, then rolled over, burying his face against the vinyl.

"Okay, that does it." Marti scooped him from the floor, carried him into his room and placed him in the playpen.

"No more fits!" She closed the door on a long, pitiful wail and headed back to the kitchen table. She stared at the paper-strewn table and poured another cup of coffee. Her cell phone said it was 10:30 in the morning, way too soon for a fifth cup of coffee.

She had bills to pay which called for an artful shuffling of money. They had been doing alright for a while, especially while Grace was here. Grace had been able to pay a couple of bills, relieving part of the burden. But now, Grace was gone and she had to pay bills as they came in and hoped for the best. Now, there was Chase McGraw Investigations to consider. A second on the small house she salvaged from the divorce? She only hoped the house was worth what she thought, or she'd be paying Chase McGraw a few dollars a month for the foreseeable future.

Chase McGraw.... She sat back and sipped her coffee. The man was too perfect with his unruly dark-brown hair, blue eyes and heart-stopping smile. She had caught herself thinking about him several times during the day at the most inopportune times.

The bedroom door cracked slowly open and a small tear-streaked face looked toward her.

"Gamma?"

"Yes?"

"Pwees, wanna horsey. Okay?"

Marti scanned the table and set her cup on the sink board. *What the heck? Things weren't going to collapse any worse than what they already had. Besides, what's the worse they can do to me? Lock me in jail for not paying my bills?*

She knelt and held out her arms. "Come here, baby."

Matthew darted toward her and buried himself against her breasts. "Oh, I love you so much," she said, showering him with kisses, then rolled him to his back on the floor for a good tickling.

"There," she said wiping his nose and the tears from his face. "Laughing is a lot better than crying, isn't it?"

"Uh-huh."

"Come with me to the table and we'll call Mrs. Adams and see if it's alright for us to come see her horse." Matthew wiggled into her lap while she dialed her cell phone. Janice Adams answered on the third ring.

"Hello?"

"Hi Janice, this is Marti. Hold on for a second. I have someone here who wants to ask you something."

"Okay."

Marti held the phone close to Matthew's face.

"Okay. Mrs. Adams is on the phone. Ask her about the horse."

The boy sat silent, staring at the phone.

"Go ahead and ask her," Marti said.

"Hello? Is this Matthew?"

"Uh-huh," he said with a head nod.

"I thought so. What do you want, baby?" Janice asked with a chuckle.

"Wanna horsey."

"Well, can Grandma bring you here?"

Matthew pulled away from the cell phone to stare at his grandmother. Marti giggled as she put the phone to her ear.

"I hate to bother you, but is it okay for us to drop by for a few minutes Your horse is all he'll talk about.

"Sure, come join us. He'll get to see some real working cowboys today. We're getting some cattle ready for market."

"Oh, he'll enjoy that," Marti said, not knowing if the statement was true. "We'll be there in a few."

She hung up the phone and studied her grandson a few seconds. "Well? Let's pack a few things and go see the horsey."

******

Marti turned through the gate and stopped to stare. There were several pickup trucks with horse trailers attached, and four cowboys were separating cattle in a paddock next to the barn that had been empty the day before. Janice was seated on the top rail, pointing and talking to one of the cowboys. Marti parked and took Matthew out of the car seat.

"Hang onto grandma's hand really tight, so we don't get lost or hurt. Okay?"

She held his hand firmly as they approached the paddock.

"Well, howdy," the cowboy said with an easy smile. "Looks like we've got ourselves another cow-puncher. Come here, son." He reached through the railing and lifted Matthew in his arms. "What's your handle, anyway?"

"Horsey!" Matthew yelled as he pointed toward one of the cowboys on horseback.

"Yeah, that's a real good hoss. The boy's got an eye for horse flesh. I'll say that for him."

"That's Matthew you're holding, and this is Marti Black, his grandma," Janice said. And I'm sure you're dying to know who's holding your grandson," she said to Marti. "This is Walt Rogers. He's one of the best team ropers around."

"Pleased to meet you, Mrs. Black." He shook Marti's hand in a gentle but firm grip.

"He got to sit on Mrs. Adams' horse a few minutes yesterday, now he won't talk about anything else." Marti said.

"Ah," Walt said with a nod and handed Matthew to her. "Sounds like me when I was his age. He's hooked. Guess I should be doing what the boss lady's paying me for." He turned away, and then looked back over his shoulder.

"I'm sure you already know this, but you might want to stir clear of this pen while we're inside. Things move a little quick in there and that young puncher might get hurt."

"Yes, thank you Mr. Rogers."

"Come on,' said Janice. "I've already got Easy saddled and ready to go." She led them toward a smaller pen.

"Horsey!" Matthew yelled and pointed.

"Yes, there's the Horsey," Janice said as she opened the gate. "Easy, come," she said and the horse walked to her side and stopped. "Okay, grandma, climb on."

"What? Me? No, no, no! I've never ridden a horse in my life."

"You're kidding."

"No, I'm not. I've lived in town all my life and was never close to a horse."

"Well that's just not right," Janice said with a laugh. "You live in the Country Music Capitol of the World, home of Merle Haggard and Buck Owens, and have never been on a horse? Everybody living around here should ride a horse at least once. Climb aboard."

"No...Really. I wouldn't know how." She looked past Janice as Chase pulled his dark blue pickup into the yard and parked it next to her car.

"I'm serious," Janice said with a grin. "I've got work to do, and if you want that little boy to sit on my horse, you climb up there first."

"I..." she muttered and stared at Chase as he stopped beside his sister.

"Got ourselves a problem?"

"Marti won't climb on Easy and give her grandson a ride.

"That's not true. I've been trying to tell your sister that I don't know how to ride a horse." A pink hue rushed to Marti's cheeks.

"Oh, gotcha," Chase said as he entered the corral. He walked around the horse with a smile that melted her insides and patted his neck. "Well, you couldn't learn on a better horse. They call him *Easy* because he *is* easy. So, climb up and sit a few minutes. I'll get the step stool for you."

It took a couple of minutes for her to get enough courage to sit on Easy's back. Chase checked the cinches and stirrups.

"You and Janice are about the same height, so the cinches are fine."

"You bet they are," Marti said. "Now, how do I get down?"

"In a minute." Chase hoisted Matthew up in front of his grandmother.

"Now, let's take one lap around the pen." He held Easy's reins and started forward.

"Ah...ah ..."

"Relax," Chase said. "We're just going for a walk, nothing more.

Marti gripped her grandson tightly as they circled the pen. But he didn't stop when they got to the end.

"Uh, Mr. McGraw. I need to get down."

"I know. I decided the boy needs a longer ride. Do you want down?" he said to Matthew. "I didn't think so," he added as Matthew shook his head. "Besides, I want to talk to you. I was going to call you, but you saved me the trouble."

"Really? Did you find something about Grace?"

"Well, yeah...a little."

He stopped the horse and reached to take Matthew from her arms. "Whoa now, no whining," he said when Matthew's bottom lip poked out. "Let's let grandma get down and I'll put you back on."

He handed Mathew to Janice then spent a few seconds admiring how Marti's Levis fit her body as she slid to the ground. He quickly coughed and cleared his throat.

"Now, admit it. That was a pretty easy way of learning a little about horses."

"Yes it was, and I want to thank you. What did you learn about Grace?"

"Well," he reached for Mathew, "for one thing. You didn't tell me she had a boyfriend." He looked at the little boy eye to eye. "Hang on tight."

Matthew squeezed his arms around Chase's neck and clung to him like a burr as Chase swung a leg over Easy's back. He placed Matthew on the saddle in front of him and trotted the horse several laps around the pen as the boy giggled.

"Okay," he said as he brought Easy to a halt. "Let's take a break. I need to talk to your grandma, okay? Then, we'll get back on for another ride."

"You two go on inside the house and talk. I'll take care of Matthew." Janice swung up on Easy's back and reached for the boy. "Go on now," she said with a nod of her head. "I've got to check on a couple of things. He'll be okay. I'll take care of him."

Marti watched as Janice walked Easy from the pen with her grandson seated in front of her. She guided the horse to the large paddock to where Walt Rogers was and stopped to talk.

"Come on, we do need to have a chat," Chase said as he took her arm.

******

"I'm sorry. I didn't particularly like the man," Marti said.

"Why not?"

"I don't know."

"There was just something about him you didn't like? Is that it?"

"Yes."

Chase leaned back in his chair tapping the desk with a pencil.

"I can't see where it's important if I liked Kirk Randall or not. I don't think they were really boyfriend and girlfriend...if you know what I mean. They studied in the student lounge together and drank coffee."

"You may not realize it," Chase said with a crooked grin, "but they have you listed as a suspect."

"No...they never said anything about me being a suspect."

"Oh, they did, in their own way. It's right there in the file." He tossed the paperwork in front of her. "Read it for yourself; it all has to do with you not liking Kirk Randall."

"Well, that's just silly! Who, in their right mind, would ever believe I would do away with my own daughter? I couldn't...really, if I was going to get rid of anyone, it would have been him."

"It happens every day." Chase leaned back in the chair, tapping the desk. "And, a good portion of the cases where it happens have to do with a family member not liking someone close to another family member. What else aren't you telling me?"

"Nothing, really."

The back door opened and Janice led Mathew into the office. The boy's pants were dripping wet.

"We had an accident, grandma. Are you almost finished? I've got to get back out there."

"Yes, go ahead. I'll take care of him."

"Okay."

Marti knelt to give the boy a hug. "Let's get your stinky clothes changed and we'll see the horses some more."

Chase waited while Marti cleaned the boy and stuffed the dirty diaper and clothes into a plastic bag.

"You're not the first person I tried hiring to find Grace."

"Yes, I know. You tried to hire Richard Lopez. He's pretty good, but he's also very expensive." Chase grinned at her.

"Yes, I know that now. He sent me a bill for talking to me over the phone for fifteen minutes."

"Did you pay ?"

"No, he didn't do anything. Why should I pay him for nothing?" Marti sat cross-legged on the floor looking up at him. "What did you find?"

"Nothing, and that's the problem. People just don't vanish, especially when they are driving a perfectly good vehicle. Unless I can find some information on her, I'm certain this case is not going to end well." He stared as Marti fastened the tabs on Matthew's clean diaper and looked slowly toward him as tears ran freely down her face.

"No, don't tell me that. I hired you to find her and you tell me this? Don't you dare tell me that."

"Mrs. Black..."

"No! Don't tell me that! She's alive and well. She's, she's just lost or being held prisoner and can't come home."

She was almost on the verge of hysteria, causing Chase to leave the desk and kneel in front of her.

"Come here." He reached for her but she pushed him away.

"No...go away!"

"Come here," Chase said and turned to Matthew. "Grandma's got an owie, and we've got to make it better."

Marti quit fighting and allowed herself to be hugged.

"God," Chase said quietly as he rocked her back and forth. "Marti is hurting real bad, down deep inside. Heal her God. Bring peace and comfort. And give her the ability to think clearly. We ask this in the name of Jesus."

Chase held her and rocked her until her sobbing quit. Matthew wormed his was between the two, trying to hug his grandmother around the waist. Chase handed her a box of tissues and crossed the room to stare out the window and watch the activity in the paddock. He didn't know why, but holding Marti Black felt right. She seemed to fit like his old pair of boots or the blue and white cowboy shirt Janice had been begging him to throw away.

Marti pulled several sheets of tissues from the box and handed the box to Chase. She wiped her eyes and blew her nose without saying a word. *Yeah*, he thought, she had stirred something inside that he hadn't felt in a long while. Not since Rita, and with Marti sitting in front of him, Rita felt like a million years ago. But there was an issue he hadn't even considered. It wasn't whether Marti Black had actually killed her daughter, or if her daughter was even dead. The problem was finding what did happen to Grace before someone in the D.A's office decided to bring charges against Marti Black.

Chapter 11

Marti checked on Matthew who was lying inside his crib. Chase had taken him on another horseback ride, and he was totally exhausted and fast asleep by the time they arrived home. She changed him once more and fixed him a grilled cheese sandwich with chicken noodle soup from a can. He fell asleep after half the sandwich, so she tucked him into bed and finished the sandwich herself, then went to her room. She slipped into her pajamas, pausing long enough to stare at her reflection in the mirror.

"You idiot," she said to herself as she buttoned the top. She would be turning forty and no one had given her a second glance that she knew of. Especially when they discovered Matthew was her grandchild. Outside of talking with several policemen, Chase McGraw was the only man she could remember actually talking to. Oh, there was the checkout man and the bagger at the supermarket, but none of them was the slightest bit interested in having a relationship with an older woman like her.

She had been pretty, at one time, and had been ogled more times than she would care about guessing. That was about the time when Charlie Black had come along and stolen her heart. They dated for four months, just long enough for him to talk her into getting married. That was her sophomore year at U.C.L.A., where she was majoring in physics. The plan was for both of them to keep attending school and graduate in the same class. That was the plan, but she got pregnant with Grace right away. That didn't seem to be a problem at first. It was a good conversation starter, and she was invited to all the parties.

Then Grace was born and things changed quickly. The party invitations quit coming. No one wanted a crying baby at their parties, so she agreed to stay home and take care of their daughter. Charlie, however, kept attending the parties and coming home late. Soon after that was when she discovered he had at least two girlfriends as well.

She crawled into bed and stared at the novel she had been trying to finish. What a joke their marriage had been. One year, three months. That must have set some sort of record. She left college completely and moved back to Bakersfield where this run-down house her parents had owned was waiting. Being what she had considered Christian, she split everything down the middle with Charlie, including the bills. Fortunately she landed a job at the local Ford dealership and hired a babysitter.

Marti started attending the same church she had attended when she was a child, but things were different now that Grace was born. They became instant celebrities of sorts. She was invited to join a Bible study group the first Sunday, but it turned out to be a study on the failing morality of the nation, aimed at her it seemed. A couple of young men had asked her out on dates, but neither of them could control their hands. She eventually quit attending altogether.

Marti replaced the bookmark and set the book on her nightstand. "Mama, I wish you and Dad were still here. I miss you both so much."

She turned out the lamp and rolled over. Almost instantly she was dreaming of Janice Adams' cattle ranch. Matthew smiled and giggled from the back of Easy. Then there was Chase McGraw seated on Easy holding Matthew. Then she was on Easy with Chase's arms around her. She woke when Matthew crawled across her body and wormed his way under the comforter to cuddle.

"Hi baby," she whispered, kissing his head. The sun was shining brightly through the window and the clock on the nightstand said it was 8:30.

Chapter 12

Grace stared as the keys rattled and the steel door swung open.

"Quit your belly-aching and get in there." A large, hairy man pushed in a small African-American girl who landed face-first on the floor.

"Okay, all of you, get inside," a redheaded man yelled. "This is going to be your hotel for the night. You might be staying an extra day."

Grace closed the copy of *People Magazine* she had been reading and laid it on the coffee table. There were six girls, with none of them looking over fifteen or sixteen years old. Grace slipped quickly to the African-American girl and gently laid a hand on her shoulder. The girl jumped with a quick intake of breath.

"Shhh, come with me," Grace said. The girl followed her to the sofa and curled next to Grace's body.

"Who's she?" The hairy man pointed toward Grace.

"She's mine," Cody snapped. "She's not with the rest."

"I'll bet the boss would like to know about her," the hairy man said. "She looks older than the rest, but she's not bad looking." He came toward her and Grace made sure she stood between him and the girl.

"Oooo, you've still got some spit left, don't you. I'll bet I can take it out of you real quick-like." He drew back his hand but Cody stepped between them.

"I said she was mine, Kyle. She's not with the others."

"Is that a fact?"

"Yes, that's a fact. Don't make me remind you again."

The two men glared at each other before the redheaded man swatted them both on the backs. "Hey, hey, you guys. We're all friends here, right? Come on, the girls are taken care of for now. Let's go grab a beer."

"Yeah," Kyle said with a smirk. "As long as Cody buys the first round."

"I'll stand you the first round, as long as you buy the next."

The men left the bomb shelter, locking the door behind them. All the girls crowded as close to Grace as they could. Not knowing any of them, and having never been in charge of a bunch of girls who were possibly being sold into slavery, Grace said a prayer. Then she took them around from room to room, allowing them to pick their own beds and take showers. None of them had any luggage or extra clothing, so she helped them pick from a bag of discarded clothing to wear while she tossed their things into the washing machine.

"Well, Cody did bring a couple of bags of groceries the other day," she said, opening the refrigerator. "Sliced cheese, butter, milk…" she began as several girls crowded close.

"You really aren't with those guys, are you?" the African-American girl said.

"No I'm not. I graduated from college and was on my way home. I have a two-year-old son I'd like to see. Anyway, I wound up here."

"What are they going to do with us?" one of the girls asked.

"I don't really know." Grace shook her head slowly. I think you might be sold. I don't know where or when…but that's what I think is going to happen.

44

The room grew quiet as Grace started some grilled cheese sandwiches. "I want to go home." One of the smaller girls started to cry.

"We all do," said another as she hugged her.

"Oh, dear Father in Heaven. Help these girls. I don't really know what's going to happen to them, but I believe it's evil. Help them all, in the name of Jesus. Please Lord, help them."

Two days later the girls were gone. They took them at eleven o'clock at night. One of the girls got punched hard by Kyle because she wouldn't quit crying. Grace spent the rest of the night praying for them.

Chapter 13

Grace removed every drawer and checked the cabinets thoroughly, looking for anything to protect herself with. Visions of those girls being herded up the stairs and into an idling delivery van still haunted her. She had spent the entire evening praying, begging God to send protection and save the girls. By what should be five o'clock in the morning, according to her watch, she had resolved that she would go down fighting if one or more of the men decided she should go with the other girls.

She made a pot of coffee and started her search. There was nothing inside the kitchen except flimsy plastic eating utensils. She returned the drawers to their proper place and moved to one of the bedrooms. Finding nothing inside that bedroom that would help, she put everything back like it was and moved to the next.

Cody brought breakfast at eight o'clock and sat at the table while she nibbled at her sausage, pancake and egg meal.

"So, where did those girls go?"

"I don't rightly know. Somewhere out of the country, from what I understand."

"You capture some girls, hold them prisoner, then sell them to the highest bidder, and you don't know what's going to happen to them?"

"No, I didn't capture anyone but you, and I didn't sell you to anyone. If you remember, I told Darrel you weren't for sale."

"So, I guess that makes it all right, doesn't it?"

The crease between Cody's eyes grew deeper as he got up from the table.

"I'm not proud of everything I do, but I gave those girls a place to sleep and fed them. They wouldn't have had any of that if it wasn't for me. And," he pointed a finger at her, "most of them were out walking the streets, selling their wares anyway. So, things aren't going to change that much for them. So don't go around preaching any of that Bible stuff to me."

Chapter 14

Grace Peterson woke and stumbled into the small bathroom to splash cold water on her face. The old Valvoline Motor Oil clock on her wall had quit running some time ago, so she had no idea if it was day or night. Her only connection to the world outside was the small marks she had made with a pencil on the wall behind the table. According to them, she had been locked inside this cage for almost four weeks. She exited the restroom and looked around.

Last night's food tray was sitting on the small table near the center of the room with one chair. A leftover piece of hamburger bun was old and crunchy. She could use a cup of hot coffee, but didn't want to cause any needless contact or conversation with her captor. Several girls were forced into the same room with her a few nights ago…at least she guessed it was night…then were taken away a day later. They had talked some, and several of the girls cried and begged to be let go, but no one listened.

She slipped quickly to the far side of the room as the keys rattled in the door handle and the door swung open.

Cody Waters entered the room carrying a tray. "I brought you some coffee, buttered toast, a scrambled egg and piece of sausage." He exchanged the trays then backed away toward the door.

"How long are you going to keep me like this?"

"Oh, there isn't any reason you need to stay cooped up like this."

"Then let me go! I have a little boy to take care of. Please, I need to go take care of him!"

"Yes, I know all about your boy. I saw his picture inside your wallet. I'll bet he's real smart."

"Let me go," Grace yelled. "Why didn't I leave with the other girls?"

"Those men thought you were too old. See those girls are young and most of them don't have families. Two of 'em are only thirteen. Besides, I told them you weren't for sale before they even got here."

He set the empty tray on the edge of the table.

"I would let you go, but you're really angry with me now, and the first thing you'd do is go to the sheriff's office and tell them a bunch of lies. Then they'd haul me off to jail when I haven't done anything wrong."

"You haven't done anything wrong? You're holding me captive, locked up in this prison with no one to talk to. All I wanted you to do is fix my car!"

"And I did that. It runs real good, and I even washed and waxed it for you."

"Fine," Grace said, placing her hands on her hips. "Let me out of here and I'll pay you."

"We'll talk about it later. I've got some things to do."

"Don't leave me locked in here," she screamed as he closed and locked the door."

Chapter 15

Marti followed Chase McGraw out to his truck, trying to balance a wiggly Matthew in her arms. Chase had delivered some copies of things inside his file that he had promised her a couple of days earlier.

"Look through them thoroughly and let me know if you can think of anything...I mean anything at all."

"I will Mr. McGraw. Thank you for doing this for me."

Chase opened the truck door and slid his Bible to the passenger seat before sliding inside.

"May I ask you something?" she asked.

"Sure, what is it?" Chase started the engine and adjusted the air conditioner.

"I've seen you carry that Bible everywhere. Do you actually read it?"

Chase blinked at her a couple of times and picked up the Bible.

"Do I read this?"

"Yes, I see you carry it everywhere, but I never see you read it. Do you actually read it, or is it for looks?"

"Well, the answer is yes. I do read it. I've got another Bible on my nightstand that I read. Do you have one to read?"

"No, I used to, but I got out of the habit when a bunch of Christians decided my daughter and I weren't quite good enough to attend their church."

"Really?" Chase turned the engine off and opened the door.

"I didn't mean to disturb you, Chase. I just wanted to know, that's all."

"You're not disturbing me, Marti. But I would like to hear more." He grabbed the Bible and slid out of the driver's seat. "Do you mind if we sit on the porch for a few minutes?"

"No, we can do that."

Chase followed her to the porch and spent the next half-hour discussing the Bible as God's word for a modern world. He confided in her a little about his former drinking problem and how the Bible helped him win the victory over a bottle of Scotch.

"Do you have a Bible in the house?" he finally asked.

"Yes, I do have a Bible. I only threw away their Bible study guides, but kept the Bible. My mother gave it to me a long, long time ago."

"Good, good," Chase nodded, "I'm glad you have one. Do you know where it is?"

"Sure, wait right here and I'll get it for you."

Marti was gone about five minutes before she returned with one of the largest Bibles Chase had ever seen. Case thumbed through Marti's Bible, finding an entire section on different Bible studies, a concordance and list of archaeological discoveries and maps.

"Wow, your mother must have loved you. This is an expensive Bible."

"Yes, she did. I guess she still does. I can't always tell," she said with a sad grin. "Her Alzheimer's kind of gets in the way."

"Where is she?"

"In Paradise Care, here in Bakersfield. I haven't seen her a whole lot after Grace disappeared."

"You should." Chase handed her the large Bible and grinned. "Take this and read some of it to her. Maybe sing her a song while you're at it and let me know how she acts."

"I tried, but Matthew kind of takes over."

51

"Let me know when you plan on going and I'll take care of Matthew."

"Are you sure, Mr. McGraw? Matthew can be a handful."

"Oh, Matthew and me are saddle pards. We'll get by. Believe me, staying in touch with your mother is important; please take the Bible and read to her."

Marti stood at the curb watching Chase McGraw drive away, wishing with every cell in her being that he would have stayed longer. *Yeah, right, Marti Black,*" she said to herself. *As if he'd be interested in you. Get real.*

She turned and walked back to the house, nuzzling Matthew to make him giggle.

******

It was two days later when she finally called Chase and said she was going to read to her mother. Chase dropped by with Buster and was in a rousing game of *Catch Me If You Can* as she drove away. To make the contest more interesting, Chase was allowing Matthew to make up the rules as they went.

Marti checked in with the nurse's station then pulled a chair close to her mother and started reading from the book of Luke. After about fifteen or twenty minutes she stopped. She had no idea how long her mother had been listening, or even if she was actually listening, but her mother was staring at her with kind, adoring eyes when she finished.

Marti spent the next eight minutes telling her mother all the latest news without mentioning Grace's disappearance. She kissed her mother and promised to return in a day or two. One of the nurses followed her to thank her for the Bible reading and mentioned that her mother's neighbor in the next bed had listened and seemed to like it too.

Chapter 16

"What I really want to know is exactly how close you and Grace Peterson were."

Chase was sitting in Kirk Randall's apartment in Phoenix with a tape recorder running and a notepad in his hand.

"Close? We were study partners. That's about it. Why?" Kirk asked as he set two cups of coffee on the table.

"Well, the Sheriff's Department has you listed as her boyfriend. I'm just trying to get the record straight. You're sure that's all you were?" He studied Kirk's reaction as he asked the question.

"No, that's all we were…not that I hadn't thought about it some." He removed a framed photograph from the bookshelf and handed it to Chase. "Have you seen her?"

Chase studied the picture for a few minutes.

"Yes, she's certainly pretty. Did you let her know your feelings?"

"Yes, I did. I told her I loved her."

" How'd she take it?"

"Let's just say it took her several months before she'd let me kiss her. She said she needed to graduate first, then maybe. But not now."

"What about her son, Matthew? Did you ever meet him?"

"Oh, no. I asked a couple of times, but no deal. She said she didn't want her son to get attached to someone who wasn't going to be around."

"Smart woman," Chase said with a grin. The questioning went on for over an hour with Chase asking questions, then re-asking the same questions couched in a different way. The answers were always the same. Chase finally shut off the recorder and closed his notepad.

"Well, I think that's about all we need. Thanks for your time." He shook Kirk's hand.

"That's okay. Anything I can do to help you find Grace. She became a Christian, you know."

"No, I didn't know that."

"Almost a month ago. I took her to a Bible study and she accepted Christ into her heart."

"That's interesting. No, I mean it's really good. One final question," Chase asked at the door. "What do you think happened to her?"

Kirk stood frozen in thought for a minute. Finally he said, choking back a sob, "I don't really know, but I know it wasn't any good. I think someone nabbed her."

"What makes you say that?"

"She wouldn't leave that little boy this long unless she was dead or being held captive. She loved him too much."

"I happen to agree with you." Chase turned away but stopped at Kirk's voice.

"Mr. McGraw? If you find her, give me five minutes with whoever did this to her before you turn them over to the police."

"I might do that, if I get the chance. Have a good day."

******

Chase pulled his truck through a Burger King drive-through and ordered a hamburger, fries and a cup of coffee. He parked in the parking lot to scan his notepad and eat his lunch. Nothing made sense. His findings were almost identical to what the Sheriff's Department had, which left him with nothing to go on. She left the college and should have been able to eat dinner with her son and mom. But somewhere along the way, Grace Ann Peterson had vanished.

"You're missing something, numbskull." He stuffed the last of the burger into his mouth, wiping his fingers on a paper napkin. "People don't just disappear. They get nabbed like Kirk said, or die in an accident or end up in a hospital. They don't vanish."

He paused as he tossed the empty containers into the trash. His doctor had told him to cut down on the cheese burgers and fries because his cholesterol was high. Maybe, but they tasted good.

"Cases like this will make you believe that aliens abducted her," he mumbled as he started the truck and pulled into traffic.

Chapter 17

Grace had almost exhausted every possibility trying to find anything that would make a weapon to defend herself. It seemed Cody Waters was very good at his job and had left nothing. The only pair of scissors were designed for children and made of plastic. There wasn't even a fingernail file or clippers anywhere to be found. Finally, on top of a shelf inside a closet, she found a wire clothes hanger.

"Thank you Jesus," she said wiping the dust from the wire hanger against her Levis. It wasn't much, but it was something. And if what she had heard in one of the Bible studies Kirk had taken her to was right, a dusty wire hanger was more than enough. After all, if Jesus could feed over five thousand people with a piece of fish and two loaves of barley bread, no telling what he could do with a clothes hanger.

She took the hanger to her bedroom and began the arduous task of straightening the hanger. When it was almost straight she took one of the pots from the kitchen and began tapping on the hanger. It took most of the afternoon, but she had the wire almost perfect by the time she knew Cody was due to arrive. Hiding the wire between her mattresses, she returned the pot to the kitchen and went to the restroom to wash up. By the time he did arrive, she was seated on the sofa reading her Bible.

"I hope you're hungry," he said, setting two plastic bags on the table. "I got you a foot-long tuna sandwich with Sun Chips."

"Thank you, Cody. I was getting tired of hamburgers and fries."

"Huh," he said as he sat down and stared at her. "Are you still mad at me? You don't act mad. What happened?"

"Yes, I'm still angry at you and those other guys, Cody. It's going to take a long, long time getting over what you guys are doing."

She closed the Bible and came to the table.

"I just can't understand why anyone could keep someone else locked inside a room when they haven't done anything wrong, then sell them like dog or cat, or...an old rusty bicycle. Tell me how you can do that, Cody."

Cody squirmed in his chair as he fidgeted with his wrapping.

"I don't know. It's just a job, like working on a car or truck. I've never given it much thought." He shrugged.

"I don't know when I've been so angry with another person, Cody." Grace stared at her sandwich bag and shook her head. "It's *not* like another job. Especially selling them to become sex-slaves. I really, honestly believe it makes God angry."

"Really?" Cody smirked as he took a bite of his meatball sandwich. "If that's true, then why doesn't he do something about it?"

"I'm sure he eventually will. The problem is you're going to be involved in whatever he decides to do. Are you ready for that?"

Cody took another bite and chewed quietly, staring at the blank wall behind the sofa.

"That wall needs some kind of picture to break up the white."

"Yes, it does. But that doesn't answer my question. Are you ready for whatever God decides to do when that time comes?"

"I can't answer that right now." He shoved the uneaten sandwich back into its bag and stood up. "I don't think about things like that very much."

"Why not?"

"Because thinking about it has never done me any good. It just confuses me."

"You'd better think about it, Cody. Whatever God decides to do isn't always pleasant. In fact, it's just the opposite. It might be time you asked him what he wants you to do."

"Maybe so, but I don't really believe God exists. In fact, I think a lot of the stuff inside that Bible you spend so much time in reading is just a bunch of stuff someone wrote to make people behave a certain way so they can get what they want."

"Oh no, it's so much more than that." Grace stood up to look at him. "God is real...more real than you and I talking right here inside this room."

"You can believe what you want, lady. But let me tell you about all the foster homes where people raised me. How I wore the old ragged hand-me-down clothes while their kids got the new stuff. I could tell you about the kids at school who made fun of me because I was so tall and skinny, or I stuttered when I talked. I worked hard to stop stuttering, and I don't do that anymore, but you know what? No one cared. Not one person said 'way to go' or 'congratulations.' You want to know why...? Because they didn't care about me. I could tell you about the time I got beaten with a belt because I took some money that didn't belong to me, because I thought I could buy some friends."

"I'm sorry you were treated that way, Cody. But not everyone is like that. My father left when I was a little baby, so I know something about what you're feeling."

"No, you don't know a thing about how I feel. You've still got your mother and a little boy. I had no one. No mother, no father, no brothers or sisters. Try living like that and see how you like it.

Cody turned and walked to the door before fishing the keys from his pocket.

"So, don't go telling me a bunch of junk that's inside that book, because I'm not interested in hearing it."

"I'm sorry Cody. I really am. But if you feel that way, why'd you kidnap me? You must have seen the Bible lying on the passenger seat."

"I don't know why I took you. I don't do that. You're the first and only one I've taken. My job is to take care of and feed the girls they bring. I took you because you were pretty and talked nice to me. I don't know. Somehow I thought you might be different and might actually like me, if you got to know me. But now I don't know if you'll ever like me."

"I can't answer that right now, Cody."

"I know you can't."

Cody Waters turned and left without saying another word. Grace nibbled at her tuna fish sandwich for a few minutes before laying it inside the refrigerator. She knelt beside the coffee table and began praying for Cody Waters' salvation more than anything. This was the first time since she had accepted Christ into her own heart that she felt woefully ignorant of God's word and the steps needed in leading someone to the Lord. It was time she got serious about knowing Jesus.

Chapter 18

"Sure, I remember seeing a woman that looks just like that. Just about our age," The kid wore a dirty apron and a San Francisco Giants cap.

Chase adjusted himself on a stool inside a run-down dinner with "EARL'S" painted in the window. He had stopped in a small desert community near highway 58 hoping to use the restroom. Then on a whim, he ordered the fish and chips that were posted on their menu board. The sign said *fresh* fish but how fresh could it be in the middle of the Mohave Desert? He asked and the kid in back said they came from a local fish farm that morning.

"She ordered a grilled cheese burger and fries," the kid said. "She never told me her name."

"Her name was something Biblical," a chunky girl with brown hair spoke up from the soft drink machine. "I don't remember what it was. Something like Love or something like that."

"Something like Grace?" Chase asked.

"Yeah," she said excitedly. "I think it was Grace."

"Take a look at the picture and see if that's her."

"Sure, I think that's her," the girl said. "Is she in some sort of trouble?"

"Trouble? Nah," Chase said with a laugh. "She's actually missing and her family is trying to locate her. Do you know where she might have gone?"

"Sure," the boy said. "She said her car was overheating, and she wanted to know if there was some sort of a mechanic around here. So, we sent her next door to

Cody's Towing." The kid pointed at the window toward the rundown building next door. The building once had been painted white and still had some white appearing in patches around the door and the window facing them.

"Really?" Chase said with skepticism. "Is he any good?"

"Cody? Sure, I think he can fix most anything, given the time." The boy dropped Chase's french-fries and fish into the deep fryer. "Of course, he makes a living towing folks who break down on the highway, or crash their cars."

"Hmm." Chase raised his eyebrows and took a sip of coffee.

"Something wrong?" the girl asked.

"Wrong? Nah," he chuckled. "I was just wondering why the Sheriff's department didn't have Cody's towing listed as a witness."

"Want me to go ask him?" the girl asked.

"Nah, it's probably not important anyway. I'll check with him before I leave."

"Here's your dinner." The boy slid a plate stacked with fish and french fries in front of him. "Your garlic bread will be finished toasting in a minute." He slid bottles of catsup, cocktail sauce, tartar sauce and vinegar in front of him.

"Can I get you anything else?"

Chase bit into the fish and found it tasty. "No, this is actually good the way it is. You've got a talent as a fry cook. My name's Chase McGraw." He shook the kid's hand.

"Thanks. I don't get to hear that much around here. My name is Earl Dean, and Susan is my wife. We're glad we could help."

"You have. At least I know she made it this far." He ate in silence as he took things in. The little diner he was in was old and had some peeling paint on the exterior, but it was a far cry from the condition of the tow shop next door. The really sad part was it was already four-thirty and besides two small kids who came in wanting ice cream cones, he was their only customer.

"The fish was really good, but how do you keep your doors open?" he said as he paid his bill.

"Oh, people don't start arriving until after five or five-thirty. They've got jobs and stuff, you know," Susan said with a grin. "We've got around twenty or thirty who eat here every day."

"Well, that's good. But it should be more."

"Thanks, come again," Earl said with a wave as Chase reached the door. He opened the truck door and stared at the tow shop for a couple of minutes.

"Might as well," he said as he closed the door and walked briskly toward the building next door.

******

"Yeah, I remember her." The tall, lanky man craned his neck to view the photograph in Chase's hand then turned his attention back to the carburetor he was working on. "A green Honda. She said it was over-heating, and she wanted me to see if I could fix it."

"Did you?"

"Did I what?"

"Fix her car."

"Yes, I fixed it. Then, while I was working on her car, some friends of hers pulled in and she takes off and doesn't pay me."

"You're kidding me," Chase said with a chuckle.

"No, and I still haven't been paid."

"What about the car? Did she just jump in and drive it away?"

"No, I've still got the car."

"She left without her car? What was she going to use for going to work?"

"It's not my problem."

"Where's the car now? Do you know?"

62

"I've still got it. It's right out back. Wanna see it?"

"Sure." Chase followed him around the building to a small impound yard. Grace's car was parked near the locking gate gathering dust.

"There it is," Cody said. "Too bad in a way. Going away and leaving it like this."

"How's that?" Chase said.

"If she'd waited a few minutes, she could have driven this car home. All it had was a stuck thermostat. I replaced it and it runs real good. Now," he wiped his hands on a shop towel, "if she doesn't come back to collect it in a couple of months, it will go up for auction. If you find her, you might tell her that. I hate it when people leave things making me responsible."

"Well, Cody, you've been a real help," Chase said, shaking the man's hand. "It makes me wonder why the Sheriff's Department didn't have any of this in their file."

"You'll have to ask them that, because I sure don't know."

******

Chase sat in the truck waiting to merge onto the highway. He grinned, thinking of the possibilities that this case was starting to turn over. Of course it all might very well mean nothing. Things like this happened all too frequently. The wayward daughter or son just pops up on the front porch with no explanation, wanting to pick up their lives where they left them. Or they climb into their friend's car and end up getting arrested in Tijuana and finding out you don't necessarily get your one free phone call in a Mexican jail. He had heard of one U.S. sailor who got thrown into the Mexicali jail and was listed as AOL for over a year. The Navy found him when the MPs went to the same jail to pick up a different sailor. Evidently the jailor didn't like the first guy and wouldn't let him use the phone.

Chase stepped on the accelerator and the diesel engine growled as the truck found its place in traffic.

Of course, there wasn't much in this case that made any sense. Grace was an absentee student, taking all her classes online and passing them easily. Some professors want their students to take their finals at the college itself, so he couldn't fault Professor Kirkland. And for all the oil under Bakersfield, he fully believed Kirk Randell was telling the truth, and what he said earlier that day matched the information inside the Sheriff Department's file. What didn't make any sense at all was Grace climbing into a friend's car while the mechanic was repairing her car that moment, and not showing up on her doorstep a few hours later. All this called for another visit to Bob Thornton's office tomorrow. He guessed it was about time he bought Bob's lunch anyway.

Chapter 19

Grace rummaged quickly through every drawer in the kitchen, finding nothing that looked like it could help. She slammed the drawer she was working on and opened a cabinet door. Nothing but pans…all sorts and sizes of pans.

"One thing's for sure, Cody Waters, if you every decided to learn how to cook, you'd have more than enough pots and pans."

She backed away from the cabinets and scanned the wall. A small red box sat atop one of the cabinets. "Aha!" she shouted and drug a chair across the room to reach it. Bounding off the chair she snapped open the plastic lid and dumped the contents on top of the table.

"Oh, Lord no!" Grace backed away from the table. "Fishing lures? Who needs fishing lures in the middle of the desert?"

The rattle of keys in the lock caused her to back against the wall. The door swung open and Cody entered. A smile slowly crossed his face as he stared at the cluttered table.

"Well I'm glad you discovered something to keep you busy."

"Fishing tackle? Are you serious? Who needs fishing tackle in the Mohave Desert, Cody?

"I love to fish," he said casually as he began repacking the kit. "But, to answer your question, I don't know. The tackle box was already here. The previous owner must've liked to fish. But," he paused to grin at her, "I don't know where."

He snapped the lid closed and studied her for a couple of minutes. "Come here. I want to show you something." He walked halfway toward the door and stopped to look at her.

"Come on. I'm going to show you about this door. Things like, how to remove it and things like that."

"Why?"

"Huh?" Cody said.

"Why would you show me how to remove the door? I thought you wanted to keep me locked inside."

"I do, for the time being. But I think you need to understand the door. Come here and I'll show you."

Grace walked slowly to stand beside Cody as he pointed with a small screwdriver.

"This door has four sets of hinges. That's because it's so heavy. The steel coating," he tapped the door with the screwdriver "is bullet proof. You could shoot it all day long and it wouldn't hurt it. But," he swung his arm in an arch "since the walls are all concrete, if you fired a gun, the bullets would bounce all around you, and maybe kill you.

"Now, on an ordinary door, you'd just unlock the door and be on your merry way. But since I hold the only set of keys, that's impossible. Of course, you could also remove the hinge pins and remove the door that way. But each hinge has a set-screw," he pointed with the screwdriver, "which means you'd need an Allen-wrench to do that, and I keep those upstairs inside the shop.

"But something I haven't told you is, this door, and the one behind it, are both filled with concrete. If you could remove the pins and pull the door out of the frame, there's no way you could hold it by yourself. It takes two grown men to handle it. So, I'd be careful if I was you, because you might hurt yourself."

"You are cruel. You know that, don't you?"

"No, I don't mean to be, especially with you." He gently caressed her cheek.

"You are cruel. You took away every ounce of hope I had."

"I didn't mean to be."

Chapter 20

"You're kidding me."

"No I'm not. It's right here." Chase waved his file under Bob's nose and grinned.

"Let me see that." Bob grabbed Chase's file and skimmed the last few pages, then reread them again.

"And you say Grace's car is still there?"

"Yeah," Chase said with a nod. "I took a couple of pictures of it. They're right there, in the back of the file."

"It's right there in plain sight?"

"Well, I wouldn't go that far. To see it, you've got to go around to the rear of his building. That's where he's got it locked inside a fenced-in impound yard. It's stocked mostly with wrecked or disabled cars."

Bob Thornton picked up the telephone. "Sarah? Call Steve Roberts and tell him to get to my office now! What do I mean by now? What kind of a question is that? I mean for him to get his sorry backside in here now. I also need the D.A. to give me a ticket to impound Grace Peterson's car and park it in our yard. No, we didn't find it…Chase found it."

He slammed the phone against the desk and glared at Chase.

"It's a sorry time when a private eye can find a car sitting in plain sight and the County Sheriff's office dances all around it."

"I didn't mean to get Steve in trouble," Chase chuckled.

"You didn't do anything, but I do expect my men to do their jobs."

His phone buzzed and Bob answered it with a "Yeah. Send him in."

"You wanted to see me?" Steve Roberts opened the door and poked this head inside.

"Come in and close the door."

"What's up?"

"I'll tell you what's up." Bob slid Chase's file across the desk and pointed. "He found Grace Peterson's automobile while you and your partner drove right by it at least twice."

"Really? Where's it at?"

"Parked at the rear of Cody's Towing, Chase said. "Inside the locked fence. It's kind of hard to see it, unless you're at the back."

"The thing is," Bob growled, "The D.A. is supposed to be cutting an impound ticket, and I want you and a driver to go and tow that car to our yard first thing in the morning. That car's evidence."

"Cody Waters thinks he's a mechanic and said he repaired her car. He will probably want to get paid before he lets it go, Chase said."

"He can send me a bill, and he'll get paid when everyone else does." Bob climbed out of his chair and arched his back. "Is that clear enough?"

"Yes, sir," Steve said and disappeared out the door.

"Are you ready for lunch?" Chase asked when it looked as though Bob had calmed himself.

"Lunch? It's only eleven-thirty."

"It's lunchtime somewhere, that is unless you don't want any."

"Who's buying?"

"I'm buying, but that's up to you. Do you want it now or later?"

"No, I am getting kind of hungry. Sarah?" he yelled as he grabbed his hat. "Chase is buying lunch today. What do you want to eat?"

Chapter 21

"Hello?" The female's voice sounded joyful, like she'd been laughing.

"Mrs. Black?"

"Yes, is this Chase McGraw?"

"Yes it is. Am I disturbing something?"

"I'm feeding Mathew his supper."

"Oh. What's he having?"

"Spaghetti, and you should see him."

Chase chuckled as a vision of a spaghetti-laden child popped into his head.

"Yes, I wish I could see that. Take a picture."

"Did you find out anything today?"

"Yes, actually I did. I located Grace's car." The comment caused her to catch her breath. Her voice quivered as she spoke.

"Where is it?"

"It's in an impound yard in a spot along highway 58 called Jackass Springs. I don't know if that's the real name, or something someone painted on a sign to draw attention."

"How did she wind up there in…where did you say?"

"Jackass Springs."

"Now I remember telling her to stop there when she said her car was over-heating. Where's Grace?"

"That's something I haven't figured out yet, but this place is connected. I can feel it in my gut. The mechanic who has her car said…"

Chase spent the next half hour explaining every detail of the day to her. She told Matthew to hold still while she took a picture of him with her cell phone then wiped Matthew with a wet wash cloth before placing him on the floor.

"There you are. Come with grandma and let's watch Barney."

"Boy, I'll bet that's fun."

"If I left him in the kitchen, he'd be right in the middle of the spaghetti he dropped on the floor. Then I'd have to clean him all over again."

"The voice of experience. This is where you need Buster. He'd lick the floor and Matthew both clean for you."

He was quiet until the sound of Barney's voice came over the telephone.

"Okay, now what's next?" she said.

"Well, the Sheriff's Department is going to impound the car tomorrow morning and bring it to Bakersfield. Then, they'll send a forensics team to go over it to see if there's anything that will tell us where your daughter is. And I'm sure they're going to ask you to identify the car as belonging to Grace. Are you up for that?"

"What? Telling whether or not the car belongs to my daughter?"

"Yes."

"What's wrong with it? Was it in some sort of an accident?"

"No, no, no. It's in perfect condition."

"Well then, of course I'm up to identifying her car. Did you find anything from the people you interviewed?"

"Not much, although I really don't think Kirk Randall had anything to do with Grace's disappearing."

"How do you know?" she almost snapped.

"His mannerisms and the answers to the questions I asked. Did you know he was taking Grace to Bible studies?"

"No, I didn't."

"He said she accepted Christ and became a Christian."

"Really? I...I didn't know that either."

"He also asked if he could have a few minutes along with whoever did this to her."

"What for?"

"I'm guessing to extract a little revenge. My guess is that he's having a little trouble with the *turn the other cheek* commandment. But the way he said it makes me want to do it, even if the law frowns on it."

Chapter 22

Grace folded the wire hanger in half and began working it back and forth. It took a while before it came apart. She hid one of the pieces between the mattresses and folded the piece in her ssshands again and began working it as before, back and forth. By the time Cody arrived with lunch she had four equal pieces of wire.

"You look kind of beat. What have you been up to?" Cody's comment caused her to glance at a mirror hanging on the wall. Her hair was askew and she had a smudge on her cheek. One glance at her hands revealed the beginnings of a few blisters.

"Actually, I've been cleaning." She dampened the corner of her paper napkin and wiped the smudge from her cheek.

"Cleaning? I cleaned this place myself just about two weeks before you showed up," Cody said with a snort.

"Cody," Grace patted his wrist, "there's cleaning, and then there's cleaning. Evidently, my cleaning standards differ from yours."

"Well, what is it that I didn't do a good job on?" Cody stood. "I want you to show me."

"It doesn't matter that much, does it? I mean once I'm gone, who's going to know what I cleaned and what you cleaned."

"I will know. Now, come on and show me."

"After we eat." Grace sat down and began unwrapping her lunch.

"You aren't going to show me?" Cody stood over her with his hands on his hips.

"Yes, I said I would." Grace eyed him slantwise. "But I'm also hungry and want to eat. Is that okay?"

"Sure," Cody nodded as he sat across from her and unwrapped his lunch. Grace carefully guided the conversation to the old Caterpillar tractor Cody said he was working on. By the time they finished lunch, Grace knew what part of the shelter she would show him. She led him to the third bedroom and into the closet where she had found a dusty area on the top shelf.

"Oh that," Cody snorted. I didn't figure anyone would ever use these closets. They don't normally come with a lot of luggage. Anyway, why are you concerned with this bedroom? Like I said, no one's gonna use it."

"Well," Grace sat on the edge of the mattress and stared at him through watery eyes.

"I get bored, Cody. I'm stuck in here with no one to talk to and nothing to do. I think I'm going nuts. Can you understand that?"

"Sure…sure, I can understand it. I'm sorry I asked."

Cody Waters left her alone the rest of the afternoon and Graced busied herself with the closet, making sure it was cleaned exactly the way her own mother would have been proud of. Then she turned her attention to the rest of the bedrooms. When Cody returned at six o'clock, the rooms were ready for inspection. Cody walked through, giving the bedrooms a military inspection and nodded his approval.

"Nice; very nice. Your standards do exceed mine. Now, let's eat. I brought tacos."

Cody's tacos turned out to be from the drive-through at Taco Bell in Mohave, but Grace had to admit they were a welcome change compared to the sandwiches and hamburgers she normally got. They ate and talked, mostly about whatever Grace chose to discuss at that moment. It wasn't until Cody was ready to leave that he gave her the news.

"I got word this afternoon that you'll be receiving company sometime tomorrow. There will be five girls this time, and I don't know how long they will be here. So, anyway, you won't be alone and will have someone to talk to for a while."

Grace sat staring at the door long after he left. The very thought of what those girls were going to go through made her ill. She also knew it was only a matter of time before someone would buy her as their sex slave and she would wind up somewhere in a foreign country where they didn't speak English. She would never see Mathew or her mother again. And, without some sort of a miracle from God, there was absolutely nothing she could do about it.

A dam burst inside her as she lay across the table weeping. *"God – oh God. Please, please help me. And help those girls that will be here tomorrow. I can't do this by myself. Help us!*

Chapter 23

"Well, what do you think, Mrs. Black? Is this your daughter's automobile?" Bob Thornton asked. "Aah! Please don't touch anything. We haven't dusted for prints yet," he added as Marti reached for the door handle.

"Sorry," she said and slowly circled the car before nodding.

"Yes, I believe this is her car.

"You're sure," Bob said.

"I'm positive. I put this scratch on the fender, so it's Grace's car." Her voice sounded weak.

"Okay," Bob said to a team of two men and a lady, "y'all heard the lady. I want to know every inch, inside and out. Let's get to it."

He turned and walked silently out of the impound yard. Chase took Marti by the arm and followed.

"What is he doing?" she asked as they joined the crowd waiting for the light to change.

"Who, Bob?"

She nodded.

"He's thinking." He looked at her and grinned.

The light changed and they crossed the street toward the Sheriff's Department.

"He gets like this whenever he's deep in thought." Chase shrugged. "Sometimes it only takes a few minutes, but I've seen it take several days. When it takes that long, I just stay out of his way, or I might get my head bitten off."

The door to the Sheriff's Department closed behind Bob Thornton before they reached it, and Chase scurried to reopen it just in time to see Bob's brown boots disappear up the flight of stairs.

"Where are we going now?" Marti asked.

"To his office to see what our next move is going to be. He'll try brainstorming us first, and then throw the ball toward us. That might take several tries, but we'll eventually have some sort of a plan by the time he's through."

He held the door to Sarah's office open for her and chuckled.

"Don't look like that. It usually works."

"He's waiting for you," Sarah said with a nod toward Bob's office. The door was standing wide open.

"Thanks."

"Close the door," Bob said as they entered the office. Chase closed the door and they both took a chair. "So," he said matter-of-factly, "where do we go from here? It'll take a few days to get the full report on Grace's car, and no telling what we'll find."

"You're not going to find much to go on."

"What do you mean we won't find much?" Marti said.

"I'm just saying the truth. Did you see the interior? Our mechanic friend Armor-All'd the interior for us. The car's been wiped clean."

"You think so?" Bob said.

"I know so. I caught a good whiff of it when they opened the doors."

"So you're not thinking we're going to find much from the car." Bob said.

"Then we won't know any more than we already do." Marti looked on the edge of despair.

"Oh no, we know a lot more than we knew when we started this case."

"Such as?" Bob said.

"According to Mechanic Cody Waters, Grace's Honda was over-heating…"

"It was," Marti interrupted. "She told me over the phone that night."

"So, then what happened?" Bob asked.

"According to Cody, he replaced the thermostat. And while he was doing that, a carload of Grace's friends pulled in the parking lot and she jumped into their car and left with them. Then she never returned to pay her bill or get her car out of hawk."

"Oh no!" Marti shook her head. "Grace always paid her bills meticulously. And she would never leave her car. She needed it to get around Bakersfield. She just wouldn't run off and leave it anywhere."

"I think that's what Chase is trying to say," Bob said. "But it really didn't happen that way, did it? Got any idea what part he's leaving out?"

"Yeah, like where Grace is."

"Maybe the young couple running the restaurant knows something," Marti said. "You said they remembered seeing her."

"Maybe, but I doubt it or they would have told me. I think the secret is lying with Cody. Just getting him to admit it is going to be the problem."

"Maybe me showing up with a couple of deputies might loosen his tongue." Bob shifted in this chair.

"It might. Let me take Marti first. Maybe if he sees Grace's mother it might help to loosen his tongue. Then," he shrugged, "if that doesn't work he's all yours."

Chapter 24

Chase pored over the missing persons file inside one of the interrogation rooms at the County Sheriff's office. He skipped over the ones that dealt with men, as well as older women above the age of thirty. He also skipped over the ones who had an active profession as prostitutes, because he firmly believed the people they were dealing with were catering to sick men who wanted a sex life with children.

He next began weeding down the list, looking for names of the victims and the dates they were reported missing. He then made a list of missing girls by area. It wasn't any surprise to discover the largest number of missing young people were in the Greater Los Angeles area. That called for a large coffee and a telephone call to the L.A. Police Department's Missing Persons unit.

Getting to talk to a live human was a chore Chase was not prepared for. He was placed on hold for forty-five minutes the first time, then another thirty-two minutes the second time. One young-sounding guy who acted as though he was going to help changed his mind once he discovered Chase was a P.I. Finally, after another thirty-minute wait, a tired sounding woman came on the line.

"May I help you?"

"I sure hope so. Who am I talking to?"

"My name is Edith Walker. How may I help you?"

"My name is Chase McGraw, and I'm working on a missing persons case in Bakersfield. I noticed that most of the cases dealing with missing kids happen to be in your area."

"Yes," she drug the word out. "I'm afraid that's true. Every time we do find and help one of them, a new batch seems to take their place. A lot of the ones we've helped go right back to the street. It's like trying to fill a hole that can never get full. So, I'll ask the question one more time. How may I help you?"

Chase spent the next hour and a half explaining his problems with Grace Peterson's case and listening to what Edith Walker had to say. Chase leaned back in his chair rubbing his eyes.

"I'm not just spinning your wheels, Mr. McGraw. First of all, the amount of kids walking the streets is astronomical. Over 1.3 million kids hit the streets every year, and a handful of police officers and social workers are supposed to solve the problem."

"Wow," Chase said. "You'll have to excuse me, but this is the first real missing person case I've had."

"Really?"

"Oh, I've had to run down a couple of wayward husbands behind on their payments and a couple of missing kids who weren't really missing. But I've never had one like this. In my days with the Sheriff's Department I worked with criminal activity."

"Well, if what you've told me about Grace Peterson is correct, you've got your hands full. I'd say she's either dead, or locked away somewhere. She might even be out of the country. Of course, you already knew that, didn't you?"

"Yes, but I don't want to tell her mother that."

"None of us do. I would go back to the last place you tracked her and chip away. You might turn over the correct rock."

Chase heaved a sigh then chuckled.

"Well, thank you very much, Miss Walker. You've just confirmed exactly what I had planned on doing."

"You're welcome, Mr. McGraw. If you'll leave me your email address, I'll send you more information as I think of it. But it is a hard and almost impossible task. Just remember, most of these kids don't know it until they hit the streets, but they are trading one hell at home for a deadly one on the streets. Best of luck."

"And the same to you, Miss Walker. God bless."

Chapter 25

Janice pulled her dusty four-wheel drive truck into the SaveMart parking lot as a space opened near the door, so she took it. She grabbed her purse and stared at a blue Ford Escape parked next to her. "Hmm." She raised her eyebrows and climbed from the truck. She pulled a shopping cart free from the line of carts jammed together near the door and entered the store through the produce door. She saw Marti Black checking a bag of apples while Matthew helped himself to a small bunch of bananas. He looked up as she approached and pointed.

"Horseys, Gama. Horseys!"

"Well, hello to you too," Janice said with a laugh.

"Oh, hi," Marti said as she placed the apples into her cart. "I'm afraid you'll always be the horse lady."

"That's okay. I've been called a lot worse." She leaned to give Matthew a kiss on the cheek and he latched onto her shirt with both hands.

"I'm sorry honey, but you're strapped into the cart. You'll have to let go."

"Let go of Aunt Janice's shirt, Matthew," Marti said.

"Why?"

"It's the store rules," she said. "Little girls and boys need to be strapped into the cart."

"Why?"

"I'll tell you what," Janice said, squatting to look him in the eye. "Why don't you and Grandma come to the ranch for dinner tonight, and you can see the horses again and maybe take a ride on one? Okay?"

Matthew released his grip with a loud "Okay."

"Oh, thank you, but we can't do that."

"Nonsense," Janice said. "There's plenty of food, or there will be once I finish shopping."

"It's not that. We've been coming to your house to ride the horses and eating quite regularly. We need to stay home once in a while."

"I can appreciate that," Janice tossed a bag of potatoes into her cart, "but we enjoy having you. You and Matthew are part of the family now."

"Thank you for saying that." Marti tossed a bag of salad mix into her cart. "But we've got to be a nuisance, eating at your table as much as we do."

"No more than having Chase or Walt sitting there. You and Matthew eat less and you clean up your messes. Besides, there's plenty of men to go around, but no women to talk to. Believe me, you'll be doing me a favor. After listening to Chase and Walt every evening, I need some good girl-talk to wash my brain out." She turned toward the butcher's station.

"You probably know what I'm talking about. Matthew's a great little guy, and I wouldn't trade him for all the cattle in the world. But there are just some things you can't tell him that you can share with another woman."

"Well, yeah..." Marti said slowly. "If you put it that way, sure. Okay, we will be there, but only if I get to bring something."

"Grab a carrot cake. Both men love carrot cake."

"Well, what do you know," Marti laughed. "I finally found something that Chase and I both agree on."

"Oh, guess I'd better call Chase and warn him he's got grill duty tonight." Janice grinned as she pulled her cell phone from her pocket.

Chapter 26

Chase crammed his notes and paperwork concerning Grace Peterson into his folder and bounded down the stairs and toward his truck. In the old days he would have crossed the other street toward the Mexican restaurant and a waiting margarita or two, but not today. Standing in front of the disciplinary board was one of the most embarrassing events he had ever endured, especially when it came to explaining to Janice why he'd been let go. She had always looked up to him, and it made him feel lower than a lizard. He prayed every day he'd never have to do that again.

He unlocked the door and slid into the hot truck. As he started the engine he set the air conditioner on high. He rolled the windows down and his cell phone rang.

"Hello, Chase here," he said without checking the number.

"Hello, Janice here." She said with a giggle.

"Oh, hold on a second." Chase rolled the windows up and lowered the roar of the air conditioner. "What's up?"

"We're at Save Mart and I was wondering when you were coming home."

"I was getting ready to head home right now. You need me for something?"

"Yes, I'm getting several salmon steaks and I need you to grill them." He could hear a child's shrill voice in the background.

"Who's with you?"

"Oh, it's just me, Marti and Matthew."

"No Walt?"

"Walt's still working, but he'll join us for dinner. Why?"

"I can grill your fish, but so can Walt."

"Walt's great at burning a good steak, but for the price I'm paying, I want this salmon half-decent. So you'll do it?"

"Yep, I'm on my way."

Chase backed out of the parking stall and turned right out of the parking lot. He had planned on giving Marti a call anyway, so her being there would save him the trouble. The problem was how to do it. What's the proper way to tell someone you can't find their missing daughter? When he was with the Sheriff's Department there were several times he'd been handed the duty of informing the family that one of their loved ones had been killed in an automobile accident or in some other way. He had never found a good way of doing it. He had left their home feeling like the lowest kind of vermin you could think of. Bob Thornton never seemed to have much of a problem telling someone their son, or daughter, or father was dead.

"It's just part of the job, Chase. You tell them then leave. You didn't kill their kid. They just died. That's all."

A dead loved one was one thing. You knew what happened and where they were. What he had to do now was worse. He had tried...he really had *tried* to find her. He had gone over and over the information inside the Sheriff's packet and personally interviewed everyone several more times and come up empty. Now he had to figure out a way of telling Marti Black that her daughter, Grace Peterson, had become part of a one and a third million person group and was really, really missing and he might not ever find her. It might be good to call a halt to this investigation. Either that, or prepare yourself for what you might, or might not find down the road. It might not be pretty.

Chapter 27

Chase pulled into the Save Mart parking lot and parked about a dozen spaces away from Janice's truck. It took him a few minutes to find the women, who were in the middle of the bread isle choosing garlic bread to compliment the fish.

"Oh, there you are," Janice said. "You got here sooner than I thought."

"I was already in the truck when you called. So, grilled salmon and garlic bread. What are we celebrating?"

"Do we have to be celebrating something to have a nice dinner?"

"No, but I do know you." Chase leaned toward Marti. "My sister never passes up a chance to celebrate something."

"Well, that might be true to some degree. I just know you don't always get a second chance to make something or someone special. So, it's always better to do it right then, when the idea pops into your head."

"See? I told you."

"Well, she's right. I know it was too late when Brian died in Iraq. He really was a good young man, but I don't think I ever told him."

"So there, smarty-pants," Janice said with a laugh. "Now, take Matthew with you, and you two go pick out the salmon."

"Yes, ma'am. We'll catch up with you before you're done."

Chase grabbed Marti's basket and headed toward the meat counter, answering "yes" and "uh-huh" to Matthew's questions. He chose four nice sized salmon steaks and one extra just in case someone else showed that Janice forgot to tell him would be there. He also chose a pack of hamburger patties for Matthew, not knowing if the boy liked fish or not. With the fish wrapped and inside the cart, they returned to the bread aisle, but the women had moved on.

"Ha, I guess Aunt Janice and your grandma fooled me. Do you see them anywhere?"

Matthew craned his neck then shook his head.

"Well, I don't see them either. I guess we have to look for them." They started down the aisle slowly, trying to spot the women mixed with the shoppers.

"Grandma, where are you?" Chase said, trying to make a game out of looking for the women. "Grandma, where are you?" he repeated. Chase was on his fourth "Grandma, where are you" when Matthew bounced inside the cart, pointed and yelled, "There she are!"

Several shoppers started laughing and a man pulling some canned goods from a shelf next to him said, "That is so darned cute."

"There you are, "Marti said, dumping several items into her cart. What have you men been up to?"

"We were looking for you women."

"Well, I believe I'm finished with my shopping," Janice said. Is there anything else you need, Marti?"

"Mmm, just milk."

"Well, that's on the way out. Let's go so we can eat."

******

"Grill's hot," Janice said as she entered the kitchen through the rear door.'

"And I'm about ready," Chase said as he removed the sauce pan from the stove. He had mixed his own Thai marinade of vinegar, soy sauce, honey, Chinese mustard and parsley. Chase allowed most people to believe it was his own recipe, although Janice knew he had copied it from a book of recipes written for a George Foreman grilling machine. It didn't matter either way to her. Her mouth was already watering.

Walt came from the barn grinning. He held the door for Chase and yelled. "Hey, Janice, I think that bay mare's pregnant. You might want to call the vet to come check her, but I'm almost positive."

"Really?" she said, wiping her hands on a dishtowel. "Do you know who the daddy is?"

"I'm thinking it's The Duke. They've been pretty friendly lately."

"They ought to have a nice colt."

"Yes, they should. It'll be a good rodeo horse."

******

The salmon sizzled on the grill as Chase drizzled the marinade across the top. Marti watched nearly every move as he quickly switched to the foil-wrapped potatoes, checking to see if they were done, then back again. She had never forgotten what it felt like having his arms around her the day he'd gotten rough on her inside the office. She had been changing Matthew's diaper and was kneeling on the floor when she burst into tears. Without hesitation, Chase had knelt at her side and folded her in his arms. She had fought him at first, which now that she thought about it, was silly. He was trying to be honest about the case. Finding Grace was a monumental task that had baffled the local sheriff's department. And as far as she knew, the F.B.I. hadn't done much better. Regardless, Chase McGraw's arms around her body had felt good; much more than she was willing to admit.

"It's ready; come and get it," Chase yelled. Janice grabbed a bowl filled with the baked potatoes and began rounding the table, dropping a potato on every plate.

"No, I've got it handled, just sit and enjoy yourself," Janice said as Marti started to get up from the table. Chase followed with a second platter filled with the salmon and two hamburger patties. She started to protest the size of salmon he dropped on her plate, but the aroma quickly overtook her common sense.

After making sure everyone had been served Chase slipped into the only vacant spot at the table, which was beside Marti.

"Chase, would you ask the blessing," Janice asked.

"Sure." He took Marti's hand like it was a natural thing to do and asked God to bless the food and everyone gathered around the table. He said "amen" when he was finished and released her hand.

She waited until he had taken a sip of ice tea before asking the question that she was dying to ask.

"Did you find anything new about Grace, Mr. McGraw?"

He paused from buttering his potato to look at her. "Uh, no I didn't. In fact, you and I need to have some sort of pow-wow about that tonight, after we finish eating."

"Really, what about?"

"After we eat, please?" He smiled warmly. "I always try to leave my work somewhere else instead of at the dinner table."

Matthew crawled out of his grandmother's lap and made himself at home on Chase's lap.

"Well, hello there," Chase said with a chuckle.

"Matthew? Come back over here and let Mr. McGraw enjoy his dinner."

"No, it's okay. Let him stay. I'll try to get some food into him." Chase's smile faded as he caught a glimpse of Marti's stern expression. "Really, it's okay, Marti. I enjoy being around the kid.

"Okay, but you behave, Matthew."

"He always behaves when he's around me," Walt said, as he placed some salmon in his mouth. "He's the perfect boy. Ain't that right, pardner?" He added the last part with a wink toward Matthew.

Matthew stared at Chase's plate for a few seconds before picking a bite of salmon with his tiny fingers and plopping it into his mouth. That was followed by another, then another bite. Chase grinned and ate his salad while Matthew ate almost half of Chase's dinner.

"Well, everyone just relax while Walt and I clear the table," Janice said after Chase and Marti had finished eating. "We have some important information to share with you two."

"Huh, I wonder what that might be," Marti said without realizing Chase had heard her.

"With my sister, you'll never know, unless you actually listen to every word."

"Oh, I'm sorry," she said with a giggle. "I didn't realize you could hear me."

"That's okay, but what I said was true." Chase took a sip of tea. "It could be anything from how much she made from the cattle sale to buying a new truck or tractor."

With the table cleared, Janice distributed plates of sliced carrot cake, while Walt followed with scoops of vanilla ice cream.

"Okay," Janice said as she sat next to Walt and grinned. "Now for the news." She looked at Walt with a crooked grin. "Would you like to announce it, or me?"

"Sure," Walt said, placing his napkin in his lap. He looked up and studied Chase for a few seconds before clearing his throat. "I asked your sister to marry me, and she said yes."

Chase stared back for a second or two.

"Really?"

"Yes, really," Janice said.

"Why?"

"Why what?" Janice snapped.

"Why would you want to marry an old broken-down rodeo cowboy like Walt? Why not a doctor or lawyer, or someone like that?"

"Because I know Walt's a nice, honest, hard-working man and I love him." She threw a piece of garlic bread at Chase's head and he ducked. Buster snagged the bread as it hit the ground. "And if…"

Chase started laughing and got up from the table to hug her. He was still holding Matthew in his arms, and he decided to get into the hugging act, plastering sticky handprints on Janice's blouse.

"What took you so long to ask her," he said to Walt.

"I don't know. Just kind of slow out of the chute."

Marti rounded the table to hug Janice.

"Is he always this way?"

"Yes he's always been that way, even when we were little kids. Someday I'm gonna brain him really good."

"Well, I hope your marriage is a good one. Walt seems like a very nice guy."

"He really is, and when it comes to ranching, the book that knows more about ranching than Walt hasn't been written."

******

The sun was starting to sink behind the mountains in the west as Chase picked up Matthew and held him close. The boy slipped his arms around his neck and snuggled his head against Chase's chest.

"What did he mean when he said he was slow getting out of the chute?"

"Walt?"

"Yes, Walt."

Chase followed Marti out to her car so she could buckle a very tired and sleepy Matthew into his car seat. The child closed his eyes the moment he heard the buckle click.

"It's an old rodeo adage, telling someone they are too slow to win."

"Oh," she said with a nod. "I guess I have a lot to learn. She raised up and closed the car door, then stared at him.

"Okay, Chase, what do you need to talk to me about?"

"It's just that..." Chase made a line in the dust with the toe of his boot.

"Go on, Chase. I'm a big girl, I can take it."

"Yes, I know you can."

"Then, what is it? Do you need more money? Is that it."

"No, the money's just fine. It's just that...well to be honest with you...I honestly don't have the foggiest clue as to where Grace is. I'm just guessing at this point."

"Well, I kind of thought that might be the case, or she'd be here with us. So, what is the problem?"

"I'm starting to think we're never going to find her."

"No, don't tell me that." Marti slowly shook her head.

"Marti." He placed his hands on her shoulders but she shook him off.

"I mean it. I paid you to find my daughter, not to quit on me."

"I've gone through the Department report three times. I read the F.B.I. file...all of it they would release to me, and it didn't tell me a thing that Bob Thornton's file didn't say. I've personally tried retracing Grace's tracks from Phoenix to Bakersfield twice and got nowhere. So, you tell me, Marti, what do you want me to do?"

Marti broke into sobs as she leaned against the car. "Don't quit on me, please. Nobody wants to find her. Please don't quit on me."

Chase reached for her, but she pushed him away. He finally caught hold of her on the third try and held her close in a bear hug. "Shhh, I'm not quitting." He felt guilty just saying the words, because that was exactly what he thought needed to be done. Grace Peterson's file needed to be closed and Marti needed to move on.

She had calmed herself just a little and blew her nose, then allowed her body to relax against his as she cried. He could feel her warm breath against his cheek as he smoothed the back of her head with his palm. Her dark brown hair was beginning to show traces of grey, but they looked good on her. He moved his head just a little to talk to her and her hot breath was next to his own lips. Without thinking, he kissed her lips, lightly at first, then slightly longer. Marti caught her breath and pulled away before grabbing him tightly and planting a long, passionate kiss on his lips. Then she jumped into the driver's seat and started the car and drove away.

Chase walked slowly back to the patio to help with the clean-up.

"Is she gone?" Janice had an armful of dirty plates.

"Yeah, she's gone."

"Did you two get everything ironed out?"

"I guess so. Here, give me those." Chase took the plates from Janice and she grinned.

"So, are you still working for her, or did you send her on her way?"

"I guess I'm still working for her, but I don't have any idea what I'm supposed to do."

"Well then," Janice took a white paper napkin from the table and wiped Chase's mouth, "maybe you should really pray about it and ask God what to do. In the meantime, learn how to wipe you lips after you kiss her." She held the red-tinged napkin for him to see.

"Cranberry Delight really isn't your color."

Chapter 28

Chase lay in bed staring at the dark ceiling trying to clear his mind, but nothing seemed to work. He had learned long ago that reading in bed didn't help. He had finished more than one book during a sleepless night and had to muddle through the day in the middle of a brain-fog. He couldn't say why he had kissed Marti. His only excuse was she was crying and he put his arms around her to quiet her, but that didn't work. Neither did holding her, so he kissed her, not once but twice. Before he knew what was happening, Marti had her arms around his neck and was kissing him back. A slow grin crept across his face as he remembered the kiss. She made a little "mmmm" noise as her warm body pressed against his and her lips explored his. Then, she pulled away with a shocked expression and quickly got inside her car and drove away. Chase climbed out of bed and went to his office to make a pot of coffee. *Yeah, the woman knows how to kiss, I'll give her that.*

He really didn't have a plan, but he knew he had missed something about Grace Peterson. He logged his computer online and did a search for Grace Peterson but didn't find anything that he didn't already know. Then, he did a search for Cody Waters, and other than his prison record for armed robbery, didn't find anything new. On a whim, he typed in a search for Jackass Springs and poured a cup of coffee. His computer dinged, causing him to miss the brim of his mug. He quickly mopped up the spill, sat in front of the monitor and started to read.

Jackass Springs had once been owned by a middle-aged couple named Jensen who built the barn and a one-room shack. They had plans on retiring and moving from Los Angeles, but something happened about a year from his retirement and they got divorced. Some people who knew them believed it was Mr. Jensen who had given the place the name of Jackass Springs.

The property then sat for several years before a college professor named Roy Moore bought the property in the 1970s. Roy Moore was a colorful character who seemed to fit in better with Fidel Castro than American politics which got him into trouble. Roy quickly applied for a building permit to have a bomb shelter installed, then proceeded to encourage everyone else to build one. Few, if anyone, listened to his warnings which started his downward spiral.

Roy Moore drove a Volkswagen van with flowers and peace signs painted over every inch. According to records from the sheriff's department and a colorful local reporter the account of Roy's last day went something like this:

Roy pulled off the highway and onto a graveled parking lot that extended approximately a hundred yards deep. He drove the van toward the white barn and circled to the back of the building before he stopped and turned the engine off. The only other building on the property was the one bedroom shack about twenty yards west of the barn that would make good firewood. He was exhausted and not in good health, but he was almost finished. All he had left to do now was unload the van and he could relax. He closed the driver's door and slid the center panel of the barn back to reveal a metal, bullet-proof door and unlocked it. He opened the door to reveal a thirty-six-inch wide staircase that led downward to a second metal, bullet-proof door at the bottom. He was rather proud of that second door, because it was not an option with the original design. It was his own idea and he paid dearly to have the contractor install it as an extra security measure. Roy fully believed everyone should own shelter, or at least have access to a bomb shelter in 1970. When the bombs and missiles came it would be too late.

He carefully descended the stairs, unlocked the door and swung it open to a twenty-four hundred square foot state-of-the-art bomb shelter. He could have gotten by with a smaller unit, but in case some of his students wanted to join him, he was ready. Roy stopped to clutch his left shoulder and arm as another pain hit him. He had hurt himself the day before carrying boxes of pots and pans down the stairs to stock the main kitchen area. He called his doctor in Mohave for an appointment, but he couldn't get in to see him for another two days. Roy took a couple of deep breaths and climbed the stairs.

The bomb shelter was more than a pet project with him, it was a means of survival. There was no question in his mind that someone either in the United States or in Russia would push a button any second and we would be sucked into nuclear warfare. The worst part was no one outside a hundred or so students acted as though they believed him. He felt like a prophet yelling warnings to the people of coming disaster, but no one would listen.

He would readily admit that his views on politics and the war in Vietnam had changed his lesson presentation inside the classroom. The administration at Bakersfield State College took a dim view of his actions, especially when he took several dozen students, armed with signs and spray paint, and blocked the entrance to one of the larger oil fields. The oil company lodged a complaint with the local sheriff's department and threatened to pull their funding from the college. Roy stood before the board and gave what he considered was one of his best speeches. Bakersfield, California was a big oil company town, and the air quality was notoriously bad. Plus, there were tons of stores and shopping outlets, bars and night clubs and plenty of things to do, but you needed an automobile to go anywhere, because there was no suitable public transportation. He had the impression that the board didn't listen to a word he said. At the end he got suspended from teaching until he had finished attending sensitivity classes, while the oil companies got another pat on the back.

Roy carried the bags of dehydrated mashed potatoes and dried corn down into the shelter, then returned to the van for dehydrated green beans.

With all the free time on his hands, he decided to host a peace rock concert in the city park with some local bands, and he still thought it was a great idea. It started out well, but a couple of bands from Los Angeles showed up around ten o'clock with a busload of fans and things quickly got out of control. One thing led to another until someone threw a brick at a policeman. The policeman wound up in the hospital and Roy had gone to jail. To add insult to injury, Carol, his girlfriend, packed her clothes and moved to San Diego without saying goodbye. In all the time they had been together, it never crossed his mind that her father was an executive with one of the oil companies. In retaliation, he quit the college, sold the house, liquated his retirement and pumped over a half a million dollars into a state-of-the-art bomb shelter.

He paused halfway back up the stairs to catch his breath. This time the pain was excruciating, causing him to break into a cold sweat. He leaned against the wall clutching his chest. He only had a bag of canned goods inside the van and he would be finished. Then, when the war started, he would be the one laughing instead of being laughed at. He slid down the wall and lay on the stairs gasping for breath. He allowed his head to rest against one of the steps as reality set in. He was suffering a massive heart attack at age thirty-eight. He was discovered ten hours later by a sheriff's deputy who had turned off the highway to investigate the light coming from the back of the barn. Roy was lying on the steps where he had fallen, dead.

Chase sat staring at the computer monitor for a few seconds before bookmarking the page. He leaned back in his chair tapping a pencil against the desk.

Really? Is it really that simple, Lord?

He shut the computer down and reached for the telephone. Marti and Bob Thornton both needed to hear what he'd discovered. No one up to this point had mentioned a bomb-shelter, and he doubted any of them knew one existed. He was halfway through dialing Marti's number and stopped. It was almost one-thirty. It could wait until morning.

Chapter 28

Dianna Rigsby leaned against the side of the convenience store watching as three other girls and one guy tried panhandling an older guy who was trying to get inside the store. He tried stepping around them several times before frustration took over and he pushed the boy and called them a couple of dirty names before entering the store. The store's manager came out and yelled for them to leave before he called the cops.

"That goes for you too," he yelled at her. "You've been standing there for over an hour. Now go before I call them."

Dianna picked up her backpack and wandered down the street toward a Wienerschnitzel. The store was closed so she rummaged through the trash can until she found a half-eaten hotdog and leaned against the store as she ate it. It was the first thing she had eaten in two days. Life in Bakersfield was not what she had pictured it would be. With both her biological parents dead, Dianna had quickly been gobbled up by the foster care system. Because she had trouble assimilating, she was bounced from home to home. The last home she was in had a seventeen-year-old boy who couldn't keep his hands off her. When she complained to his parents, he denied everything and she was punished. So Dianna packed what she could and raided the kitchen, taking a jar of peanut butter, a loaf of bread and a pack of Oreos.

She was smart and a hard-worker, so she thought finding a job shouldn't be too hard. What she discovered was that no one wanted to hire a fifteen-year-old girl with no address and holes in her jeans. Now the loaf of bread was gone and the peanut butter jar was empty, and she had eaten the last Oreo the day before yesterday.

She leaned against the building as several girls passed. One of them turned to look her up and down.

"This is our corner, honey. Go find your own."

Dianna picked up her backpack without saying a word and started walking. A tear trickled down her right cheek. She was alone with no job, no money, and nowhere to sleep. Even the whores didn't want her around. To top it off, there would be nothing to eat in the morning when she woke, and she had no plan. She had decided to flag down the next police car she saw and turn herself in as a runaway, but she hadn't seen one in over an hour.

A fairly new Chevrolet cargo van pulled to the curb beside her. The van didn't have any writing on the side and no rear windows. The sliding door rolled back and a huge blond-headed man grabbed her arm.

"Hey, what do you think you're doing," she yelled as she fought against him.

"Shut up and get in the van!

"Let go!"

He pulled her almost inside, but her backpack got caught on the door.

"Let me go!" She dug her fingernails into his neck and raked down.

"Ahhh!" he bellowed and hit her.

The blow opened a deep cut in her left eyebrow. The man threw her backpack out and slammed the door shut.

"Let go!" he said as the van lurched forward. She tried to get to the door but another blow crushed her lips, spewing blood on the side of the van. Then he hit her several more times as Dianna tried shielding her face with her arms, but his fists continued to rain on her as she cried.

"Oh, God! Please quit hitting me! Please – no more!"

Chapter 29

Marti Black changed Matthew and wiped his face and hands as best as she could, without fully waking him.

"Come on, baby." She laid him in his crib and covered him with a light blanket. "Pleasant dreams." She kissed him on the forehead and turned out the light.

She went to the bathroom to wash, and wound up staring into the mirror for what might have been an eternity for all she knew. Her mind and emotions were a tangled mess, and she didn't have a clue as to what she should do. Move to Alaska? Maybe she could land a job on a salmon boat. Although today's salmon experience was close to her limit of knowledge on the subject. But at least she would be free from having to face Chase McGraw.

She left the light on and went into her bedroom to fetch her pajamas. Then, making sure all the doors and windows were latched, she went back to the bathroom to disrobe and take a shower. Marti stood before the full-length mirror looking at her nude body while the water warmed. Sucking in her tummy didn't seem to help much. Her body was pushing forty years old and that was that. She had never asked, but she imagined Chase was close to the same age. He was a junk-food junkie who was built like a movie star. It was totally unfair.

She climbed into the shower and let the warm stream wash the stress and frustration of the day away. The thing the water seemed to miss was the feel of Chase's body as she leaned against him, and the feel of his strong arms as they wrapped around her and pinned her against him. The water also missed the feel of his lips as they covered her mouth. It was true he had kissed her first...twice. Her returning his kiss was the natural thing to do, wasn't it? Yes she had liked it, but did Chase enjoy it? Oh, Lord, what if he didn't?

She leaned her head against the pink shower tile and banged it like Charlie Brown from the comic strip. "Why, oh why, oh why?"

She had always considered herself to be a *take charge* woman. At least, that was what she was on her job. If the numbers didn't match, or something was missing, she checked things until they did. She fixed things. That was what was so frustrating about Grace. No one, not the Sheriff's Department, nor the F.B.I., nor even Chase McGraw could find her. But she knew Grace was still alive. She could feel it inside. It was true.

She climbed out of the shower and dried herself then slipped into her pajamas. She blow-dried her hair in front of the mirror, bending over to make her hair look fuller. Did she like Chase McGraw? Sure, she reasoned. Probably eighty to ninety percent of the women who met him fell in love. He was big, handsome and gave her the feeling he really cared, and that's what angered her. How do you love someone who won't help you find your daughter?

She lay in bed with the open Bible in her lap. She could give him kudos for getting her to read her Bible. She stared at the opposite wall for a few minutes. When she was honest with herself, yes, she did love Chase McGraw, but he worked for her and that was as far as it could go.

Lord, I'm sorry for acting improper tonight and kissing him. But please, Almighty God, tell us what to do to find Grace. Please.

Marti fell asleep with the opened Bible in her lap and the bedroom light on. It was the ringing telephone that woke her two hours later.

Chapter 30

"What happened to you?" Grace hovered over the little waif of a girl lying on her bed as she dabbed at the dried blood crusted on her swollen lip and eye. She had been alone for several days. Cody Waters popped in the morning following their conversation, delivering food, and told her there was a change of plans, then disappeared. She only saw him for a few moments three times a day when he brought food and took the trash out. The shelter was slowly becoming a dungeon, making her fight to even climb out of bed. The fact that the girls were prisoners like her broke her heart, but she welcomed the company anyway.

"What does it look like happened? They grabbed me off the street and I put up a fight. Then that big guy did a number on me, and then he laughed when I cried." She was one of six girls, counting Grace, jammed into the bomb-shelter. Grace thought the oldest might be around fifteen. There was one little girl sitting on the edge of a cot across the room rocking back and forth as she cried who might have been eleven or twelve.

"How long have you been here?" the first girl asked.

"I really don't know…three, maybe four weeks. Maybe longer." Grace re-soaked the paper towel and placed it back on her crushed lips.

"Hold that for a while. It might bring down the swelling and I'll see if there's anything I can do."

"What are they going to do to you?" the girl asked as Grace crossed the room to the younger girl.

"I honestly don't know, but I'd like to get out of here. I have a two-year-old son I'd really like to see. I don't believe they knew I was as old as I am."

"How old are you?"

"Twenty-four. My husband was killed in Iraq. After my baby was born, I went back to school to get a teaching credential. I hadn't planned on being here, that's for sure. My guess is they don't know what to do with me, or I'd be gone." Grace sat on the edge of the cot and folded the girl in her arms. The girl burst into sobs as she clung to her with both arms.

"Shhh, crying isn't going to help. We'll pray and maybe God will work things out."

Grace began rocking her and kissed her cheek several times. "You are loved, you know that? All of us inside this room love you, and someone very special loves you."

"Oh, God. Help these girls. I can't believe any of them had planned on being here, and I can't believe they want to be here either. Maybe they made some wrong choices, and maybe they've done some things that aren't right. But you can change that. Please help them, God."

******

It was about an hour later when the sound of keys rattling in the door caused the girls to stop what they were doing and stare. The twelve year-old started crying and placed her cot between her and the men. The door swung open and they entered carrying Jack in the Box bags and placed them on the table.

"You'd best eat up girls. The boss is trying to get a good price for you, and once he does, he'll want to move you real quick," Cody said.

"Where are you taking us?" one of the girls asked.

"That all depends on who buys you, doesn't it? Go on, eat up."

105

He turned to leave, but noticed Grace wiping the corner of the girl's mouth and eye, and crossed to see what she was doing.

"Is she going to be okay?"

"Maybe, no thanks to your friend over there."

"I can do the same to you." The big guy cracked his knuckles.

"Not if you know what's good for you," Cody snapped in anger. "You mess up their faces and that brings their value down. And he doesn't like not making all he can."

"Look what she did to me!" He pulled his shirt collar down to reveal several fresh fingernail marks.

"It still doesn't matter," Cody said. "He's not trying to sell *you* now, is he?"

Cody glanced around the room, making sure nobody else looked as though they'd been beat on.

"Okay, let's go."

The big man stopped long enough to grab his crotch and grin at the girl on Grace's bed. "Come on, you know you'd like your stud muffin."

Cody yelled and they left the shelter laughing, locking the door behind them. Several of the girls rummaged through the paper sacks and a couple began picking at the food.

"My name's Dianna," the girl with the paper towels said. "What's yours?"

"Grace."

"You've been here longer. What do you think is going to happen to us?"

"I really don't know for sure. Cody won't talk to me about that. But from what I've seen, you'll be here a few days, and then disappear. I'm sure you'll be sold to some rich guy somewhere in a foreign country, or here," she said with a shrug. "Then another batch of girls will take your place.

"You might get to hang around here a few days longer for your face to completely heal. In a way, that brute did you a favor." Grace choked and blinked back tears.

"It literally makes me ill."

Chapter 31

"Ahhh, you got me." Chase lay on the grass as a giggly two-year-old jumped on his stomach. Buster ran circles around them barking loudly. Marti stood by the gate to the lawn area watching the melee.

"Here," Janice handed her a cup of coffee as Walt turned the steaks on the grill. There were half a dozen rowdy cowboys seated at two of the picnic tables. A couple of the men had wives and children and had brought them with them. They had finished the fall roundup and this, along with a paycheck, was Janice's way of saying thank you.

"Thank you." Marti took the cup and smiled. "He really is pretty good around children, isn't he?" Marti said as she sipped the coffee.

"Yes, he has always been that way, even when we were kids. I'd gravitate toward kids my own size, but if you wanted Chase, you'd find him playing games with some little kids or carrying one around."

"Really? I wonder what made him that way?"

"Who knows," Janice said with a laugh. "It may have been having me as an older sister. The way we grew up living on a ranch, we didn't have any other kids to play with, so we played with each other."

Janice looked at Marti with a grin and laughed.

"I was older than Chase, so I pestered him mercilessly. The only way to get me to stop was for him to play with me, or do what I wanted him to do. And..." she drug the word out, "I never really stopped."

"Lord, I wish I had a brother like that."

"I never asked, but don't you have any sisters or brothers?"

"No, just me. Then I married and had Grace. Then I got divorced after discovering my husband had a couple of girlfriends. So, it was Grace and me. We were pretty close until she got married and had Matthew. We were kind of like *The Three Musketeers* until this mess came along."

"Well," Janice said as she turned away, "I've got a good feeling about all this." She looked back over her shoulder and smiled. "I've had my prayer team praying for you and I think it's all going to end pretty soon. Things are going to be okay."

"I sure hope so," Marti said.

"It will."

Marti looked down as a giggling Matthew darted to grab hold of her left leg.

"Oh, no!" Chase said, placing both hands on his cheeks. "You found the base, now I can't catch you. What am I going to do?"

"I don't really know about your game of tag, but Walt says the steaks are ready. Come and get it," Janice said.

Chase picked up Matthew and walked through the line holding the child, asking him to point at the food he wanted. As it turned out, the boy wanted meat and bread.

"Ha, there ain't a thing wrong with that boy," one of the cowboys said with a laugh. "I wouldn't mind having him as a saddle pard once he gets a little older."

"From the looks of things, you might have to arm-wrestle Chase for that privilege," Walt said.

Chase did sneak a spoonful of potato salad into the boy's mouth, then had to feed him the rest of what was on his plate. They finished the meal with chocolate cake and vanilla ice cream. Matthew was half asleep by the time they were done. Walt went to the bunkhouse and returned with his guitar. One of the other men had a fiddle he quickly tuned. They were about halfway through *Faded Love* when Marti took Matthew from Chase's arms.

"I'm sorry, but I've got to get this little cowboy home. We'll do our best to be back here by six-thirty in the morning."

"You don't really have to go; you know that, don't you?" Chase said quietly. "Janice has the guest room all made up for you."

"Yes, I know. But he's going to need more diapers and milk, and I'm sure some extra clothes. Besides, Janice has some chores she'd like to finish before we arrive."

"Okay, I'll see you both in the morning." Chase looked at Matthew who was now fully asleep. "Tell him I said goodnight."

"I will. Thank you for a lovely time."

"It wasn't me. This is Janice's yearly thing."

He held open the car door while she strapped Matthew into his car seat, then closed it.

"Good night, Marti. I'll see you in the morning."

"Good night, Chase McGraw. We'll be here."

He stood by the gate, watching her car disappear into the night as Janice joined him and slipped her arm through his.

"So, tell me little brother, which one is it?"

"Which one is what?"

"What you're really interested in. You spent the entire evening playing with Matthew, but I've seen how you watch Marti. So, which one is it?"

Chase stared at his sister for a quick minute before cocking his head to one side.

"Why can't it be both?"

Chapter 32

Grace closed her Bible and stared at the girls. She hadn't asked for the task, and really didn't want it, but all five of them had begun looking for her to have all the answers. The only answers she had to their plight was prayer and reading her Bible, and that seemed to be pitifully weak at the moment. Cody had come in earlier in the day to inform them they were going to be moved that evening. The move was going to be a quick one and they needed to be ready. That was when he stopped to stare at Grace.

"The order is for you too. I'm trying to talk him out of it, but the boss has found someone who wants to pay top dollar for you." He turned and left, leaving her with a block of ice where her heart used to be.

"Come here, girls," Grace said, opening her arms wide. "Let's pray."

She poured out her heart in prayer, asking not only for their personal safety, but complete deliverance from their captors. Several of the girls followed her prayer with a prayer of their own.

"Okay," Dianna said as she started looking around the kitchen, opening drawers and cabinets. "I may have to go, but I'm sure as the devil going down fighting."

"Believe me, I've been through them several times myself," Grace said. "He emptied anything we might find to fight with before I was dumped here. "But," Grace lifted the top mattress from her bed to reveal the four pieces of heavy wire. "He missed a wire clothes hanger that I found."

"Way too cool." Dianna grabbed one of the weapons. In an instant the other three pieces were grabbed.

"Okay, stuff those into your clothing until you need to use them," Grace said as she dropped the mattress. "Because they'll sure take them away from you if they see them.

"I'm not getting inside that van of theirs," Dianna said. "They'll have to kill me first."

"That's the way I feel myself," Grace said.

"What about us? What are we going to fight with?" one of the other girls said.

"Well, let's see." Grace grabbed a container of table salt from the cupboard and put it on the table. "We'll use this."

"Salt? What good is that?"

"Have you ever gotten salt in your eyes?"

"Yeah, it burns like…" the girl ended her sentence with a curse.

"When we hear Cody's keys rattle in the door, we'll each take a handful of salt, and when we get up the stairs, throw it into their eyes."

"Then what?" Dianna asked.

"Then, we play it by ear. Knock them down…kick them below the belt…take Cody's keys away and lock them inside here. God will tell us what to do."

"I hope so," Dianna said, then chuckled as she stuffed the piece of hanger under her shirt in back. "It would be a real hoot to lock 'em in here and let 'em rot." That statement brought several cheers from the group, followed by ideas of what they planned to do to the men once they had them captured.

"Okay, listen up," Grace said. "What we need to do now is be quiet and listen for Cody's keys. We'll take turns sitting near the door so we can hear them coming. Who wants the first shift?"

Dianna chose to be first, followed by an African-American girl they called Ruby then an Asian girl named

Lu. Grace guessed it might have been a little past midday when Lu jumped up excitedly.

"Shhh, I think they're coming."

The container of salt was quickly passed around as the keys rattled against the door.

"Wait until I throw my salt, then attack." Grace readied herself as the door swung open.

Chapter 33

Marti pulled her car through the gate and parked it next to the barn. The sun had just risen enough to turn the eastern sky a golden red. It was feeding time and Janice was busy pitching hay into several different feeding troughs.

"Horsey!" Matthew squealed and pointed.

"Yes, those are horsies, aren't they?"

She grabbed Matthew's diaper bag and slung it over her shoulder before unbuckling his car seat. Let's go see the horsey.

"I'd planned on having this done before you got here," Janice said as she tossed another forkful of hay into a trough. "But today I'm running a little slower for some reason." She tossed another forkful and jammed the fork into a broken bail. "There, all done. Now," she held out her arms. "Let me see my boyfriend."

"I can't believe you're doing this," Marti said as Janice kissed Matthew and squeezed him in a bear hug.

"Oh, this is no trouble at all. In fact I rather enjoy it."

"Maybe, but you won't get any work done."

"Work? Who mentioned work? We're going to play with the horses and go for a picnic. Aren't we, Matthew?" The boy giggled as she nuzzled him.

"Where's Chase? He told me not to be late."

"He was on the telephone the last I saw. Ah," she said as the rear door to the house opened and slammed shut. "Speaking of the devil, there he is."

"Sorry to keep you waiting," Chase said as he joined them. "I just wanted to check in with Bob, and I was right."

113

"Right about what?" Janice said.

"Grace's car had been wiped clean. The only fingerprints were Cody's."

"Well, good luck," Janice said, bouncing Matthew in her arms. "Tell Grandma and Chase bye-bye."

Matthew waved and received a kiss on the cheek from Marti. She climbed into Chase's pickup and placed her heavy handbag between their seats before fastening the seatbelt. Chase clapped his hands and whistled. "Buster, come." Buster ran from the barn and jumped into the rear seat. Chase shut the door and started the engine as Marti turned for another wave. The diesel growled as he turned the truck toward the gate.

"Lord it's hard to leave him, even for a minute," Marti said.

"I'll bet it is," Chase said as he pulled onto the highway. "He certainly stole my heart and I only took him for a few rounds around the exercise pen."

"Oh, I caught you playing peek-a-boo with him the other day. Then, how about the game of tag-you're-it on the front lawn?"

"Well, those were freebies. Every little boy and girl needs those on a regular basis."

He slowed the truck to merge onto 58 toward Mohave.

"Is there any reason we're taking Buster today?"

"Sure, to give him a chance to see something new. All he does is see the same old thing day after day. How would you like being stuck like that?"

"Probably not so much."

"Plus he's a pretty good tracker, when he wants to be."

Marti sat quietly staring out the windshield and listening to the gentle roar of the motor. It was several minutes before she broke the silence.

"Where do we find Cody Waters and his garage?"

"In Jackass Springs. I thought I'd treat you to some fish and chips at Earl's if nothing else."

"It sounds quaint," Marti said with a chuckle.

"It is, but the food is actually pretty good."

The truck engine growled louder as it shifted into a lower gear. Chase signaled and pulled into the fast lane to pass several big-rigs struggling to climb the Tehachapi Pass.

"You can pop a CD into the player if you want," he said. "I really don't mind. You'll find a bunch of discs in the console."

Marti flipped through the dozen CDs in the box and laughed.

"What's wrong?"

"Nothing's *wrong*," she said. "I was just going to ask what type of music you liked to listen to, but I guess it's country."

"Yeah, I'm sorry. That's all I have in the truck."

"Do you listen to any other type besides country?"

"Sure I do. Classic rock, blues, even some classical and gospel. But as I said, country's all I've got in the truck."

"Well," Marti said as she opened a jewel case, "Then you're getting Merle Haggard." She slid the CD into the player and was instantly surrounded by *Today, I Started Loving You Again.*

"I hope you don't mind, but I thought we might talk to Kirk Randall also."

"That's a long drive to Phoenix, Mr. McGraw. Are you sure we have enough time?"

"I took the liberty to invite Kirk to meet us at Earl's Diner around noon."

"No, I don't mind. And," she added as an after-thought, "I'll be on my best behavior. You said he didn't have anything to do with Grace's disappearance, and today I believe you're right. That might change down the road. But today, you're right." They rode in silence for a couple of minutes. "You are right, aren't you?"

"I sure hope so," Chase said with a laugh.

******

An hour later, after listening to more Haggard and listening to Marti read several passages of scripture from her bible, Chase slowed and signaled as he left the highway and pulled into Jackass Springs, then parked near Earl's Diner.

"Oh, my word," Marti said as she exited the truck. "This looks like a ghost town. Is there anyone here?"

"There was a couple of days ago when I ate here." Chase clapped his hands. "Buster, come!" The Border collie leaped from the truck, gave a loud yawn and stretched.

Someone started banging on a piece of sheet metal at Cody's Towing and the front door to the diner opened.

"Well, hi." Susan grinned as she poked her head out the door. "You did come back."

"Sure. I told you I was coming back."

"Yeah, but most people say that then don't. Come on in. The coffee will be ready in a minute."

"I'll be in there in a bit. I've got to make sure Buster waters a couple of weeds first."

"Do you have a restroom?" Marti asked.

"Sure do. It's right there in the far corner," she pointed. "My name's Sue and that's my husband, Earl, in the kitchen. Take your time. I'll have a cup of coffee on the table."

"Thanks." Marti hurried to the restroom and found the place neat and clean. Every aspect of the diner seemed to contradict itself. The peeling paint, the almost deserted town, yet the interior and exterior of the diner were clean and immaculate like a high-end restaurant. True to her word, Sue had a steaming mug of coffee at the corner table.

Chase opened the door and poked his head inside. "Do you have a place I can tie him?"

"Bring him in," Earl yelled from the kitchen. "What's his name?"

"This is Buster. He and I are buddies; best of friends. Are you sure?"

"Do you work for the health department?"

"No, I'm a P.I."

"Then bring him in. I'll give him a treat."

Chase seated himself next to Marti and wrapped Buster's leash on his chair leg.

"Is this your wife, Mr. McGraw?" Sue said.

"Ah, no. This is Marti Black. She's the mother of the girl I've been looking for."

"Oh, I certainly hope you find her real quick. Earl and me have been praying for her."

"Thank you," Marti said, and turned to look out the window as a new Nissan pulled into the parking lot and parked next to the diner.

"Here's your first meeting," Chase said as Kirk Randall climbed out and came inside. He took one look around before joining them at their table.

"Have you two met each other?" Chase asked.

"No, we haven't had the pleasure," Kirk said, offering his hand. "It's a pleasure to meet you, Mrs. Black."

"Sit yourself down," Sue said with a grin. "What can I get you to drink?"

"Ice tea."

"One ice tea coming up." Susan disappeared toward the back and Kirk chuckled.

"How'd you ever find this place? I passed it twice before pulling in here."

"That's their problem," Chase said. "The food's great. It's just that no one knows they exist."

Susan set Kirk's tea in front of him. "Now, let's take your orders so we can get them started. "You," she pointed toward Chase, "want the fish and chips."

"Yes, you read my mind."

"And what would you like, ma'am?"

"A chicken salad sandwich."

"One chicken salad. And what about you, sir?"

"A cheese burger with fries."

"A cheese burger. And, a free beef patty for the dog. I'll get these ordered. In the meantime, if you think of anything else, please let me know."

She headed toward the kitchen and Chase chuckled.

"She's been well trained somewhere and will make a fine waitress, if they can build a business here."

"Maybe this'll help," Marti said as a dirty Chevy pickup pull in the lot and parked next to the building. A dusty cowboy and a young cowgirl climbed out and came inside."

"Two cheese burgers with fries, Sue," the cowboy yelled as he opened the door.

"Gotcha, Frank. diet or regular Pepsi?"

"Regular."

Several more customers arrived by the time their food was delivered. Kirk took a bite of his burger and paused. "You're right. This is actually good. Really good."

Marti took a small bite of her chicken salad and nodded. "So is the chicken salad. Too bad we can't move this place to downtown Bakersfield. It would be a gold mine."

"I could be wrong," Chase said, "but watching how they talk with the customers, I'm thinking they aren't too far from being as busy as they want to be."

They went back to eating while Sue and Earl took care of their other customers. Sue saw Chase slip a couple of French fries to Buster and said "oh, I'm sorry," and rushed to the back and returned with a small bowl full of fried hamburger for the dog.

"We were letting this cool so you wouldn't burn yourself," she said as Buster gobbled the food.

"Now, that's service," Kirk said with a laugh.

******

Chase was paying their bill when Sue said "wait a minute. I have something the lady might want." She reached under the counter to retrieve a neatly folded jacket. "Grace, the girl you're trying to find, left it here hanging on the back of her chair. Then she went to see Cody and never came back."

"Thanks, Sue. I'm sure Marti will want it."

He handed the jacket to Mrs. Black then had to help her find an empty seat as she broke into sobs. He could hear Sue explain what had just happened to the other customers as he knelt beside her. Kirk pulled a chair to Marti's opposite side and sat quietly rubbing her back. Buster acted as though he wanted into the act also, and wormed his way between Chase and Marti and took several good sniffs of Grace's jacket. Chase stared at the dog as he sniffed, then stood up and stretched his back.

"Kirk, can you sit with her while I take Buster out to pee on some weeds?"

"Sure, take your time."

Chase gave Buster the full length of the leash once they reached the gravel driveway, and instead of finding a weed patch to water, the dog crossed back and forth across the lot sniffing. Every once in a while he would bark loudly and go back sniffing, working his way toward Cody's Towing shop. He could see Cody Waters, who was working on an old tractor, rise up to watch the dog.

Buster reached the corner of the building and turned right, skirting toward the back of the shop, where he started barking at the side of the building.

Cody climbed off the tractor and grabbed the largest wrench inside his tool box and followed after them. He caught up with them as Chase pushed on a sliding door. The door slid easily on well-greased rollers to reveal a heavy concrete-filled steel door.

"You don't belong here. Get back around front," Cody almost yelled.

"What's behind this door, Cody?" Chase stayed calm on the outside, although his insides felt like a trampoline.

"You don't need to know what's behind that door. I told you everything you need to know. Now, get back around front."

"I can get a court order to search your property, Cody. Is that what you want?"

"I want you to clear off my property."

"Not until I get to see what's in there." Chase grabbed the handle and gave it a jerk. The door didn't budge.

"I said, get around front!" Cody yelled as he raised the wrench high over his head.

"Okay, okay," Chase said with a slight laugh and raised his hands. "But, you might as well know I'm going to call the Sheriff's Department and get a search warrant to search your property."

"You can do what you want to do as long as you stay off my property."

"I can't search it without actually being *on* the property.

"I said…" Cody raised the wrench again and Chase almost dragged Buster away from the door.

"We're gone," Chase said as he backed away. He headed back toward *Earl's* and paused before entering. He watched as Cody talked to someone on his cell phone, pointing every now and then toward the dinner.

Chase entered the diner and smiled warmly at Marti. "Well, I know where Grace is."

Marti gasped loudly as she jumped to her feet. "Where is she? I want to see her."

Sue stopped in the middle of delivering an order to one of the tables to stare at Chase. "You found her? She's not being held prisoner at Cody's, is she?"

"Well yes, that's exactly where she is."

Chase was instantly swarmed with questions from the patrons and he had to raise his hands to get them to stop.

"Whoa, hold on for a minute. I've got to place a call to the Sheriff's Department first then I'll answer all the questions I can." The diner grew quiet as he punched the numbers into his cell phone.

"Hi Sarah, this is Chase. Can I please talk to Bob? Well, what I have is kind of important also. Tell him I know where Grace is. Yes, I'm ninety-nine percent sure. No, I'm standing here looking at the building where she is right now. Okay, I'll wait."

He stood staring at Cody's Towing through the window, tapping his foot.

"Yeah, I got him, Bob. No, the trouble is we'll need a search warrant, and it wouldn't hurt to have a couple of uniforms here when we make the arrest. No, the same place where you got her car. No, there's a false panel on the back that slides easily. Then there's a steel door that's locked tighter than a Scotsman at tax time. Maybe, but I'm Scott."

Chase listened to the phone for what seemed an eternity to Marti. She was about ready to snatch the phone and scream at whoever was on the other end.

"No, he ran me off his property once. You want me to go back and try again? Didn't think so. Okay, but make it snappy. He's still on his cell phone. I think he's trying to make connections to get rid of whoever's locked behind the steel door. Yeah, we'll wait, but make it fast. I don't want to lose her now that we found her."

He ended the call and smiled again at Marti. "I really, really believe she's in there."

She jumped to her feet and headed toward the door. Chase caught her by the arm.

"Wait a minute, Marti. Where are you going?"

"I'm going to go get my daughter."

"Not like that, you're not. Bob's bringing several officers and a search warrant right now. We're going to search that place from top to bottom legally. We don't want to make any mistakes that will let him walk out of the courtroom a free man."

"I want my daughter… now!" Marti yelled.

"I know." Chase held her tightly. "So do I. We all do."

He positioned her chair so she could watch Cody's Towing and sat beside her. The tall dusty cowboy pulled his own cell phone from his pocket and punched some numbers into it.

"Wayne? This is Joe Baxter. Is it alright if we cancel our appointment until tomorrow? Yeah, something's come up. Nah, I'll fill you in tomorrow. Okay, two o'clock tomorrow then. Bye."

He sat back and gave Sue a friendly nod. "Sue? How about a couple of cups of coffee for Beverly and me?"

"You sticking around?" she asked as she filled two mugs.

"Sure, you never know when you might need a good veterinarian."

"Really?"

"You never know. That border collie might hurt himself and need some doctoring."

"Yeah, I guess you're right." Sue refilled the coffee cups at the next table. The short heavyset man seated near Chase mumbled a curse as he stood.

"I hate to leave, but I've got water running." He stopped at the door and raised his voice. "I'll be back. Save my place."

"Okay, Smitty. I'll make sure you get a seat," Sue said with a smile.

"So, what do we do now?" Kirk asked Chase.

"We wait."

"That's it? We just sit here and wait?"

"Yes." Chase laughed. "That's how most cases are closed—by waiting."

"I think it's boring and I'm sick to my stomach," Marti mumbled.

"Yes, but it will get your daughter back."

Chapter 34

Robert Thornton hung up his call from Chase McGraw and bellowed.

"Sarah!!"

"Yes sir?" She poked her head into his office.

"Call Justice Waterford and tell him we need a search warrant for Cody's Towing in Jackass Springs on Highway Fourteen, and we need it yesterday. Chase McGraw's pretty danged sure he's found Grace Peterson."

"Really? Is she okay?"

"We don't know that yet. We don't even know if she's alive. That's why we need the warrant."

"Okay, right on it."

Bob lifted the phone as Sarah disappeared back into her office and dialed the garage. "Hey, Scotty, this is Bob Thornton. Pull my car around and make sure the tank's full and everything's good to go. Yeah, I'll need it in about fifteen minutes. You'll be getting calls from a couple of other deputies also and they'll need the same thing. Yeah, this is really important. Thanks Scotty. See you in a few."

He hung up the phone and then redialed.

"Steve, how busy are you? Well, drop whatever it is your doing and head to the garage to get your car. Yeah, and grab Candy and bring her with you. She'll need her own car. I'll try to bring another officer with me. Yeah, its right down your alley, a long drive followed by rescuing a beautiful woman. Well get on it now."

He hung up the phone and opened his lower desk drawer to remove his sidearm. By law, he was supposed to wear it at all times, but Bob had never really seen a need for it inside his office. He buckled the belt with a sigh, hoping the gun would stay inside the holster. He grabbed his hat and poked his head into Sarah's office.

"Any luck?"

Sara was on the phone and waved him off for a second. "Thank you, your Honor. Chief Thornton will be by your office to pick it up in a few minutes. Thank you, sir, and God bless."

She hung up her phone and grinned. "He's writing it as we speak."

"You're an angel, Sarah. I'll be gone for the rest of the day."

"Drive carefully," she yelled as he disappeared. "And bring that girl back alive and well."

Chapter 35

Chase took a cup of coffee from the restaurant out to his truck and dropped the tailgate. He sat on the tailgate sipping his coffee and watching Cody bounce around like a caged squirrel inside a room full of dogs. Joe Baxter came from the restaurant with his own coffee and sat beside him. He took a sip and motioned toward Cody with his head.

"He must know his time is about up. It looks as though he's about to explode."

"He is, and the longer we wait, the tougher it gets on him."

"I can tell you're pretty good at this. You served in Iraq?"

"Some." Chase sipped his coffee and gave Joe a crooked grin. "I got to watch a couple of interrogations and participated a time or two. We have some pretty incredible men and women doing that sort of stuff."

"What's the toughest part of this? The waiting?"

"Pretty much. Ol' Cody's about to come apart as it is. If you added another problem to the mix, he might blow his own brains out."

"You don't want that if you can help it. Do you?"

"No, I really don't want that. Then, I'd have to fill out a report as thick as the King James Bible and stand before a review board or lose my license. It sounds cold when I put it that way, doesn't it?"

"Yes, but that sort of thing happens to us too." Joe sipped his coffee. "In medicine, they might drag someone two-thirds dead into the hospital and you have to treat them.

If they pull through, you're a hero. But if they die, you lose your shirt in a lawsuit. That's why I'm a vet. Dogs and cats don't drag you into court. Their owners might, but not the animals and not very often."

"Yeah, I guess that makes sense." Chase jumped off the tailgate and stretched. "I've got to take a short break. Can you watch our friend and let me know if something changes?"

"Sure, take your time."

Chapter 36

Cody Waters paced back and forth inside the decaying barn, cursing himself for being a fool. He had allowed himself to be talked into this scheme, but no matter how much money he stood to make, he was certain he wouldn't be able to spend the money if he was locked up inside a prison cell.

He also cursed Grace for pulling into his garage with an over-heated Honda. From the instant he saw her she was all he could think about, especially when she smiled at him. He had only seen women with her beauty in movies and magazines. Someone needed to make a law that women who were as pretty as her couldn't wear makeup or fancy clothes.

He double and triple cursed those other girls locked inside the shelter. They were nothing but noisy, messy kids. None of them could hold a candle to Grace Peterson, but the boss wanted them. He claimed he had a buyer overseas willing to pay top dollar for them. He was planning on sending them away on a Chinese tanker soon. If that was the case, let the buyer come and get them. Cody couldn't wait to get rid of them.

He glanced at the restaurant and cursed. The private investigator was gone now, but a big lanky man had taken his place, sitting on the tailgate of the Ford pickup, staring at him inside the barn. Cody made an obscene gesture toward the lanky man and cursed. He then cast a truckload of curses down on the private investigator. He wouldn't be in this mess if it wasn't for him. He had claimed he was looking for Grace Peterson, but Cody didn't know if that was really true.

What type of an idiot would keep looking for a woman who had been missing for a month? There had to be a cut-off time on everything, didn't there? I mean, you look for a while, then when you don't find them you move on to someone else. That's the way it's supposed to be.

Cody redialed the only telephone number he had been given and let it ring. The telephone continued ringing until the automated voice on the other end told him the man he was calling was unavailable but would return his call as soon as possible, so please leave a number. That was the sixth time he had called. Cody cursed loudly and punched the rotten barn siding, knocking one of the boards lose as he realized the number he had been given was to a throwaway phone and his contact wasn't going to answer. He was going to have to handle things himself, one way or the other.

Chapter 37

Chase returned to sitting on the tailgate with an extra-large container of French fries.

"How's it going inside the barn?"

"Oh, I think you're really getting to him," Joe said.

"How's that?"

"Well, I think I've been called every profane word there is, and then some. And see that board lying on the ground?"

"Yeah?" Chase sat up straight and craned his neck.

"Well, about five minutes ago, Cody let out a string of curses and punched it, knocking it off the barn with his fist."

"Huh, I guess we might be close to having all hell break loose any minute. Want a fry?" Chase held out the box.

"Nah, not right now. This is starting to get interesting. You might want to write all this down in a book. It might make you rich."

"You'll be able to write that book when we're finished," Chase said with a chuckle. "As wired as Cody is, he's making it easy for us. Of course, it might backfire if his pancakes flip and he tries to run or tries to kill someone. It turns into a whole other game at that point."

"Does that happen very often?"

"Not very often, but I have seen it a time or two overseas. If that happens, just stay low and out of sight. I'll take it from there."

Chapter 38

One of the smaller girls named Abagail started dancing from foot to foot and bouncing up and down. "What's the matter?" Grace said. "You act like you have to pee."

"I do."

"Well, there's the bathroom. Go." Grace pointed toward the opened door. The girl sort of bounced into the room and dropped her jeans without closing the door.

"When I get nervous, I have to pee. It's always been that way."

"Well if it happens when they come for us, you might have to pee your pants," Dianna said with a smirk.

"Let's be kind girls. We're all in the same boat, and it's going to take all of us to escape."

"Well, I wish they would hurry. I'm hungry," Wendy said. "Well, I can't help it," she added when several girls giggled and laughed. "I get hungry when I get nervous."

"Good," Grace said with a crooked grin. "Now we all have something else to work for. Wendy's hungry and Abby's got to pee. Who else has something to work for?"

"I do," Grace didn't know the girl's name. She had stayed by herself and this was the first time she remembered the girl speaking.

"Great! What is it you need or want?" They all listened to her describing an itch that attacked every time her nerves acted up. She was followed by another girl.

Oh, my heavenly father, Grace prayed silently as the girls talked and giggled. *Every one of these girls was*

130

designed and created by you, and they are precious...every one. Please, my God, by your nail-scarred hands and awesome power, set us free.

Chapter 39

Kyle Boltz leaned his bulky frame back into the swivel chair and grinned. The cell phone on the desk had started ringing non-stop around two p.m. and had not stopped. Something, or someone, must be giving Cody Waters fits.

Serves him right, Kyle thought. The jerk thought he was something, but in reality, anyone could do what he did. Stick the girls into the old bomb-shelter and make sure they're fed a couple times a day. What's the magic in that? But old Cody really thought he was special. The ringing stopped as the recorded message took over.

Cody had been around long enough to know the boss didn't like them calling him during the day, especially on that cell phone. Numbers that are frequently used were easily traced, and the boss didn't want anyone to know his private phone number. Kyle was amazed the boss had gone to check on a possible target and left his phone behind.

The ringing started up again, causing him to laugh. Old Cody was probably ready to eat the paint off the side of his tow truck by now. That was good, real good. He needed to suffer a little. Calling him down in front of those girls like he did the night they dropped them off—nobody talked to him like that and got away with it. Kyle swore to himself that the next time Cody tried anything like that he'd be missing a few teeth.

The ringing stopped and the message started over. It all would repeat itself again in a few minutes.

Chapter 40

Marti came from the restaurant sipping on a diet Coke. "When are we going to make him open the back end?" She eyed Chase over the rim of her Styrofoam cup.

"We're getting close, but really, according to the law, we're supposed to have a search warrant, or nothing we find in there can be used as evidence."

"Well, if we don't get Grace pretty soon you won't need any search warrant or anything else."

"Because?"

"Because I'm going to brain him myself, even if I have to drive his truck through the door."

"Hmm, that might be worth watching. But let's hold off on the truck for a little while. Bob Thornton should be here any minute now, and he can do the braining."

"Chase has been doing great driving Cody over there nuts," Joe Baxter said with a snort. "Take a look at him. He's like a rat on speed locked in a six-inch cell."

Marti watched Cody pace back and forth, then stop to look at his cell phone and curse. Cody made several more obscene gestures toward them then went back to pacing.

"My word! He's like a madman."

"I told you so. This man knows what he's doing. It's going to get exciting when the Sheriff's Department shows up." Joe glanced at Chase and laughed. "I think I might write that book and let Bev take over the business."

"What book is that?" Marti said.

"A book on breaking down a terrorist's will," Chase said with a chuckle. "Joe said I should write one, but I told him he could do it."

"Are you saying Mr. Waters is a terrorist?"

"Mmm, yeah," Chase said with a nod of his head. "Sort of. He's not blowing up buildings and stuff like that, but they kind of think alike."

Chase waited a few more minutes before jumping off the tailgate. "Well, let's see what happens if I up the game just a little." He went inside the restaurant and returned leading Buster and carrying Grace's jacket. Chase stood where Cody could see him clearly as he allowed the dog to sniff the jacket.

"Okay, Buster. Go find Grace."

He removed the leash and gave the dog its freedom. The dog trotted across the lot toward Cody and the man literally bounced in the air, yelling.

"Get that _____ dog out of here! Now! Go on, get him out of here!" Cody ran to his tool box and came back with the largest wrench. "Get him out of here!"

Chase followed the dog, giving verbal commands as Buster skirted the barn toward the back.

Cody charged forward, cursing and trying to cut him off.

"I told you to stay away for the rear of my building. You don't belong here, and I've already told you everything you need to know."

Chase squatted and called Buster with a clap of the hands and a whistle. He replaced the leash and grinned at Cody.

"I still need to see what's inside there, Cody. And, I have a search warrant on the way. You can let me in now, or later. It's up to you."

What he got in answer was a good cussing and another threat if he didn't leave.

"Okay, Cody. Don't blow a gasket. I'm leaving and taking my dog. But I'll be back again when the warrant arrives."

Chapter 41

Grace paced the floor with an uneasy feeling inside. She was anxious about having to leave the bunker, but there was something else, like an impending war, and these young girls were her army. They didn't look too threatening, and certainly not scary, but they were what she had.

"Okay girls, let's go through what might happen. They'll open those doors and herd us up the stairs to an opened door on a van. I'll try to be first so I can start things before we reach the van. If they won't let me be first, Dianna will be in charge."

"Why her?" one of the girls asked.

"I don't know. Maybe because she's older than the rest of you. Either way, it has to be done right, because we're only gonna get one chance.

"Now let's pretend we all have our salt in our hands. I'm going up the stairs," She acted as though they were climbing stairs. "We reach the top and I yell at the man at the top and throw my salt. Yaa!"

All the girls yelled, "Yaa!"

"Throw the salt right into their faces. Now, push them down…maybe down the stairs if that's possible. Kick them, bite them, anything you can. Just take away any guns or knives and beat them senseless."

She stood back and listened as the girls chattered like a bunch of sparrows. She had no idea where her plan for battle came from, and she had some real doubts as to whether or not it would work. But, it was better than no plan, and who knew? It just might work.

A verse out of Exodus she had just read that morning came to her mind.

The LORD will fight for you, and you have only to be silent."

A warm peace suddenly filled her from the inside out, pushing away the uneasy feeling. It reminded her of being wrapped in a warm blanket on a chilly winter day.

Oh, please, Lord Jesus. Help this to work. Thank you Lord. Thank you.

Chapter 42

Bob Thornton had to wait an hour before the D.A. signed off on the warrant and made sure everything was legal and on the up and up. He then scowled at Bob, letting him know this should be handled by another office. With the warrant in his hand, Bob felt somewhat elated until the printer inside the courthouse went on the fritz. Not only would it not print, its high-speed print mechanism had eaten the original copy of the warrant and would not return it. Bob was about ready to shoot the copier when Officer Candy Martin unplugged the machine, waited fifteen seconds, then plugged it back in. The copier worked like a charm.

"If I wasn't married, I'd hug and kiss you about now," he said.

"Well, have at it." She pointed to her left cheek. "But, I'd rather have a raise."

"We might be able to work something out."

With three squad cars and four officers, Bob turned on the lights but left the siren off as they sped through the Tehachapi Pass, traveling by silent alarm. It had been awhile since his last trip across the Mohave Desert. For the most part, he had always thought it was hot, dry and desolate and not fit for diamondbacks or jack rabbits.

Dropping down to the desert floor, he exited to the right and drove through the middle of the town of Mohave. He exited right again toward Lancaster and sped back up. He radioed the other cars, telling them to keep an eye peeled, because he'd never been to Jackass Springs before. He was beginning to think they had missed it when Candy in the vehicle traveling on his rear bumper radioed back.

"I see it about a hundred yards ahead on the right."

"Yeah, I've got it." Bob flipped on his turn signal and killed the flashing lights. He pulled off the highway and parked next to Chase's pickup. The other cars parked next to him. Chase was sitting on the tailgate of his truck eating french fries.

"Well, if you aren't the poster boy for surveillance," he said as he crawled out of his car.

"Well, there's nothing happening right now," Chase said and passed the fries to Bob.

Bob took a couple and ate one. "They're cold."

"Yeah, I know. But I can only eat them so fast."

"So, what's been going on, exactly?"

"Well, for those who need a potty, they have a pretty clean one inside the restaurant. They also have great hamburgers, fish 'n chips, and breakfast." About half of them hurried inside to line up at the restroom.

"I thought so," Chase said with a chuckle.

"Now that that's settled, what's happening at the barn?" Bob asked as he jumped up onto Chase's tailgate.

"Not much," Chase said as he tossed the remainder of his cold fries into an outside trash can. "I think I kinda got under old Cody's skin."

"You did? How so?"

Bob sat quietly listening as Chase caught him up on the proceedings of the day and watched the tall, thin man pace back and forth inside the barn.

"Is that him?" Bob asked after Chase finished his account.

"Yes, that's Cody Waters."

"He looks five bottles shy of making a six-pack."

"He is ... at least from what I've seen."

Cody stopped his pacing long enough to give them another obscene gesture.

"Huh, I wonder what he'd think if I gave him an attitude adjustment when I arrest him?"

"He might not even notice if you did."

"What are we waiting for?" Candy asked.

"Well, mainly I was waiting for a search warrant," Chase said. "That's one thing he made clear. He doesn't want anyone nosing around his property without a warrant."

"Sounds reasonable," Bob said with a nod. "So the old boy knows something about the law."

"A little," Chase said. "Earlier today, I'd planned on handing him the warrant and then find out who or what he's got hidden behind that door. But now?"

"But now what?" The humor was gone from Bob's voice.

"But now, I think there's something else that's missing."

"It's a long drive to return empty-handed, Chase."

"Oh, don't worry about that." Chase shook his head. "We'll use the warrant, and we'll find someone or something of interest. I'm just saying…"

"You're saying we ought to hold off for a while."

Chase gave Bob a crooked grin and shrugged.

"Yeah…just a little while."

"Yeah, just a little while," Bob said with a snort. "And just to get it right, we're doing all this on a hunch you have."

"Yeah, that's about right. And while we're at it, why don't you move the cars somewhere out of sight. They might spook some of Cody's friends if they show up to do business."

Bob stared at the cars and nodded slowly. "Steve, you guys heard what he said. Let's move the cars."

"Where to? There's no buildings or anything around for miles."

"No, it only looks that way," Chase said. "There are mobile homes and cabins all over the place. But, if you head out on the highway going south, just past the old horse corral, you'll see a wash toward the right. People have been using it as a road, so it's packed pretty good. Pull into the wash and keep right. You'll wind up right behind Earl's Diner," he pointed "right there."

"You heard him. Let's get it done."

They waited until the deputies drove away before Bob stuck out his hand and grinned. "If we're going to do this, let's make it look good." He gave Chase's hand a vigorous shake before climbing into his car and starting the engine. "See you later," he hollered and drove away.

Chase watched the car disappear around the curve in the highway before going back inside the café. So far, the plan was on schedule to work. He headed toward the restroom praying a little prayer that nothing would screw it up.

Chapter 43

Cody quit pacing the interior of the old barn to watch the first batch of sheriff's vehicles drive away, making him wonder what was going on. He was certain they were there to cause him more trouble, but he must have been wrong. On the other hand, what were they there for if they weren't there to arrest him. He'd been in prison once and swore he would never return again. He'd die first.

He turned his attention back to the P.I. who was still talking to the big sheriff's deputy. They were acting like they were old friends, and that had Cody perplexed. Not that they couldn't be good friends and they were visiting. He was sure the P.I. had friends; most people did. But what was the deputy here for? He doubted that the deputies had driven all the way from Mohave just to say hello to him.

He glanced at his wristwatch then turned back to Chase as the deputy shook Chase's hand and climbed into his car and drove away. Chase walked casually into the café and disappeared. Cody watched the café for a few more minutes before relaxing. He crossed the barn and poured himself a mug of coffee, then drug a chair back to where he could watch the café. He was still considering that the P.I. might still be trying to trick him into making a mistake and somehow let him into the shelter.

Cody took a sip of coffee and breathed deeply. He knew the whole thing was a mistake and he should have never gotten involved, but the money was too good to pass up, and all he had to do was house the girls out of sight inside the shelter for a few days until the boss made the arrangement, then move them. He didn't have to kidnap anyone or do anything stupid like the other guys. Just food and clothing—that was all.

He took another sip of coffee. Well, he had done a real stupid thing in nabbing Grace Peterson. All she wanted was to get her car fixed so she could go home. That was what he should have done—just fix her car. But she was just about the prettiest girl he had ever seen, and he had wanted time to discover whether she could like a guy like him or not. He was certain she could by the way she acted. She had a real pretty smile and a cute laugh. But the following morning, when she woke and discovered he had drugged her and placed her inside the bomb shelter, had changed everything. He might as well have kidnapped a wild horse or cougar. And nothing Cody could do was going to change her mind. But how was he supposed to know she had been married and had a son?

He took another sip and set the mug aside as his cell phone started to ring.

"Cody's Towing."

"Well hello Cody." It was Kyle Boltz on the other end. Cody could tell the man had been laughing. "Are you being overrun with boogie men?"

"No, there were three sheriff's deputies here hanging around the café, and one of them acted like he was good friends with the P.I."

"That's good. You know the boss doesn't like to move his product when it's still light outside. There's too many people who are awake and see things."

"I know that, Kyle. I also know you guys were going to hang me out to dry, weren't you?"

"Not unless we had to, but you knew that was the risk when you took the job. Isn't that right?"

"Yes."

"Okay, then what's your problem, Cody? What can I do for you?"

"Let me know when you're coming to pick up the load. I'm kind of stuck here."

"Oh, are you getting nervous, Cody?"

"Yes, I'm getting nervous. You would be too, ____."
It was the first time he'd ever called Kyle a bad name, but Kyle Boltz was mean and he was cruel, and Cody just plain didn't like him.

"Watch it Cody, or I'm liable to run your head through one of the bunker walls."

"Give me a time, Kyle. I don't have all day."

"How about eight o'clock? Does that sound okay to you?"

"That sounds fine." Cody hung up the call and finished his coffee.

He could see the writing on the wall crystal clear. The way this whole system had been set up was to protect the next guy. Everyone had a job to do, but they didn't know the name of the guy above them, or the guy below them. He didn't know who the girls were given to. The only reason he knew Kyle was because he had met him in prison. It was at Kyle's urging that Cody had taken the job in the first place.

He had made up his mind. Cody rinsed out his mug and placed it on a shelf near the coffee pot. He would finish this job but once he had received his cut, he would be gone. He'd leave his tow truck and stuff what he could into one of the cars in the impound yard and be gone. He knew another guy he'd met in prison that could give him a new driver's license and identification card. He could make it like he was a brand new person who had never been in trouble. That would mean Grace would have to go with the other girls tonight, but so be it. If something happened and they didn't show up to get the girls tonight, he would leave the key ring lying on the counter inside the barn and leave the girls locked in the bunker. Someone would eventually show up and let them out. If not he would still leave.

Chapter 44

Grace sat the girls around the kitchen table so they could discuss any trepidation they had about what might take place that evening. They also practiced what they were going to do once they smelled clean air.

"Okay, while we're waiting for them to arrive, we need to rest and make sure we're ready physically."

"I'm hungry," Wendy said with a slight whine.

"Oh no," Dianna said with a laugh. "Here we go again."

"Be kind, girls," Grace said. "In fact, that's good. We do need to eat before they show up. We might not get a chance to eat again for quite a while. Wendy, you're in charge of the menu. Some of you other girls set the table. This will be our special dinner just for us tonight."

"Too bad we don't have something good to drink with our dinner," Dianna said.

"Oh, I think we do. I ran across this one day when I was cleaning." Grace drug a chair to the pantry door and retrieved the small jug of Carlo Rossi burgundy wine. "I'll give each of you a small taste of this with your meal, but no more. I want you to have clear heads when we go into battle. Okay?"

"Sure," Dianna said with a nod. She was followed with a plethora of *yeahs* and *cool, dudes.*

Dinner amounted to dehydrated Salisbury steak, dehydrated mashed potatoes and canned green beans. While the meal was edible, Grace vowed right then she'd never eat anything that had been dehydrated again if she could help it.

After everyone had eaten, Wendy and Abby started clearing the table.

"Uh, girls?" Grace said. "Let that go for tonight."

"Huh? We always clear the table," Abby said.

"Yes, and if you were home, or visiting someone, I'd say clear the table and wash the dishes. But this is different. We're going to be fighting for our lives, so Cody Waters or whoever is alive at the end can clean the dishes."

The statement brought a big cheer. When they all quieted down, Dianna turned toward Grace and shrugged her shoulders. "What now, Captain?"

"Now, we wait. It shouldn't be too long now."

Chapter 45

Marti grabbed Chase's arm as he passed her table inside the café. "Chase, can you please tell me what's happening? I thought the sheriff was going to give Cody Waters the warrant so we could see what's in there. But he left without doing a thing."

"No, not quite," he said with a crooked grin. "And I'm sorry, I should have been telling you what's going on. Come here and I'll show you."

He led her to the last table nearest to the highway and pointed. "Oh, wow!" she said, staring at the cars backed up against the bridge spanning the wash. "Why did they move them over here?"

"It's kind of a two-edged sword. We had them parked in plain sight just to rattle Cody's cage. Now, we've moved them to make him think the officers left and he only has me to deal with."

"Is that wise? I mean, we all know he's not really stable."

Chase studied Marti's face for a few seconds. She really was a pretty woman and, excluding the night he had kissed her, it had been a long time since he'd held a woman in his arms.

"Chase?" she said as he studied her.

"I really don't know what he'll do. I guess we have to be on our guard."

He touched her cheek with the tips of his fingers and left the restaurant. She watched as he opened the driver's door to his pickup and felt under the seat. She caught her breath as he removed a large pistol and clipped it to his belt in the back, then straightened his shirt.

"What is it?" Susan asked as she joined her at the window.

"He just strapped on a gun."

"Hmm," Susan said and nodded her head. "It must mean Cody's time is running out."

She turned and gave Marti a crooked grin.

"These walls ain't much good at stopping bullets, but they're better than nothing. So, if the shooting starts, lay on the floor until it stops."

"You're joking...right?"

Susan opened her eyes wide and shook her head. "No, I'm not. If they start shooting at each other, you'd better lay on the floor. Unless you're really Wonder Woman in disguise."

Chapter 46

Cody opened a fresh bottle of Pepsi and took a big swallow. The officer's cars had driven away without seeing him at all. He guessed whatever they were doing had nothing to do with him. He sat on an old barstool and took another swallow. The liquid burnt its way toward his stomach.

There had to be some way to pay Chase McGraw back for all the trouble he had caused him. Chase might have thought it was funny and some sort of game, but he had really frightened him. Cody glanced toward his tool chest on rollers. His large box-end wrench was lying on top. If Chase decided to leave the restaurant and come harass him about some stupid search warrant, he'd part his hair with that wrench, then they'd see how funny he thought this whole mess was.

Cody's hands shook as he tried to light a cigarette. He finally got it lit on the third match and inhaled deeply. Once he turned the girls over to Kyle and collected his money, he was going to lock the doors, climb into one of the cars out back and head north. The green Chevy ran good; he'd take that one. He'd probably switch cars somewhere around Chico. He would pay cash for it and give them a bogus address, so he shouldn't have much trouble that way. The only thing he regretted was not really mending bridges with Grace Peterson. But, when he thought about it long enough, he didn't really think it was his fault. He had tried being nice, and showing her how he felt, but she just wouldn't open up to him. So, he'd give Grace to Kyle as a bonus and let him deal with her. Then, she could see how she liked being treated by Kyle, instead of the way Cody would have treated her.

Cody tossed the butt onto the gravel parking lot. Yeah, that's what he'd do. Then, he'd have enough money to last him quite a while and not have to worry about anything. That's when his cell phone rang.

Chapter 47

Kyle Boltz finally picked up his cell phone and hit redial. He had let Cody suffer long enough. Besides, Cody had never struck him as the brightest light in the house, and no telling what he'd do from one minute to the next. Cody had been the one to come up with hiding the girls inside the old bomb shelter, and even found the remote location. But in his opinion, Cody Waters was just plain nuts.

The first time he'd seen this side of him was back in prison when several guys were standing around in the exercise yard smoking cigarettes and discussing how easy it would be to escape. And it would have been, too. But like most plans made in prison, when exercise time was over, everyone went back to their cells and forgot about it, but not Cody. He thought about it until escaping prison became an obsession with him. And sure enough, Cody got caught trying to slip out by trying to hitch a ride on the garbage truck. But the thing that amazed Kyle was, Cody was able to sling some sort of line that appeased the warden and he got off easy.

"Hello?" Cody said on the third ring.

"Yeah, you've been trying to drive me nuts by calling all day long. What's up?"

"I've still got the merchandise. Are you coming to pick it up?" Cody's voice sounded calm and collected compared to what he had been feeling nearly all day long.

"Sure, we're coming, why wouldn't we be? So, one more time. What's up?"

"What's up? Nothing's up right now, except that private investigator has been hanging around the diner most of the day."

"Really? Is he still there?"

"He's inside the diner right now." Cody glanced through a pair of small binoculars pointed at Earl's. "It looks like he's eating his supper."

"Well, let's give him time to eat, and maybe he'll leave.

"Maybe, but he might surprise you. You never know what he's going to do. It might be better if you came a little later."

"We could do that," Kyle said with a snort. "What do you think he'll do?"

"I don't know. He had several sheriff cars here earlier."

"Really? What'd they do?" He was starting to sound like the old Cody he'd known in prison, and that wasn't a whole lot of fun.

"Nothing."

"Nothing? Did they come to your shop or ask a bunch of questions?" Kyle said.

"No, nothing. They stayed awhile at the diner then left. I did see them eat around noon."

"Okay, there you are," Kyle said with another snort. "They were probably just eating lunch. It really doesn't sound like you've got a problem, does it?"

"No, I don't guess I do. Are you coming?"

"Sure, we're coming. We'll be there in an hour or so."

"Okay, I'll have them ready. Park so you'll block the view of the bunker from the café and open the hood. It will block anyone trying to spy on us."

"Okay. You just be ready."

Kyle hit the disconnect button and laughed. Cody had really slipped a wire. It was about time to get rid of him before he caused some real trouble.

Chapter 48

Cody unlocked the door to the bunker and entered, looking haggard and mostly spent. He glanced around the room slowly. All the girls were present except one. The little short one. What was her name again? Abby? Yeah, I think its Abby. He was about to ask where she was when he heard the toilet flush. Grace was cooking something at the stove that smelled spicy. It made his stomach growl.

"The girls ate earlier, but they were getting hungry, and you forgot to bring any food for them. I hope you don't mind." Grace smiled at him and kept cooking. "I made plenty, if you want to eat with us."

"No...I'll drive into town and get dinner there. You girls eat all you want."

Grace moved the pan off the burner as Abby came from the bathroom. "It's ready, girls. Come and grab a plate."

They crowded around the stove as Grace wormed her way toward Cody.

"Is there some reason you came, or do you just want to visit?"

"A visit's always nice, but no. I just got a phone call. They are coming to move you girls tonight. So make sure you're ready."

"Oh," Grace said with a slow nod. "Do they have time to eat?"

"Oh, yeah. They won't be here for an hour, maybe two."

"Okay, Cody." Grace touched his arm and nodded. "I'll do my best to have them all ready."

"And, I hate to say it, Miss. Grace. But this move includes you."

"Really? I thought that might be the case. You warned me it was going to happen. Remember? Do you know where they're going to move me?"

"No I don't know. They never tell me those things. I hate to lose you, but you need to get ready too."

There was a low roar of protests coming from the girls that Grace was included in the move.

"Now girls, I'm sure it isn't Cody's fault I'm being moved with you. We'll just have to see what God has planned for us."

"Well, that's what I had to say. I'll see you in an hour or so."

Grace sat at the table as Cody left the room. Dianna slid a plate of Spanish rice in front of her and ordered her to eat. "You'd better keep your strength up too. We have a war to fight, remember?"

"Yes, I remember. Thank you."

She smiled and chatted lightly with the girls and went over their plan of attack once more, but her insides were all knotted up.

Chapter 49

"Excuse me," Bob Thornton said and motioned toward Susan. He was seated at the table farthest from the window facing *Cody's Towing* in hopes they wouldn't be seen inside the diner and blow the stakeout.

"Yes, can I get you something?"

"What time does this place close?"

"Normally," she said, glancing at the clock hanging on the wall that said it was ten minutes after seven. "We close around six, but that all depends."

"Depends on what?"

"It depends on what's happening," Earl said with a laugh. "Like right now."

"Really?" Bob scooted in his chair to face Susan as she refilled his coffee cup. "And why is that?"

"Well, honey, this is the most exciting thing that's happened around here since we've been open."

"What does happen around here?" Candy said as she bobbed her tea bag in a cup of hot water.

"Well, besides Joe and Bev delivering a new colt or calf every now and then, not much, unless someone decides to crash their car on the highway."

"Oh, Carl Rainwater did decide to kill his wife a few years ago," Earl said as he dumped an order of fries on a plate. "But that happened before we opened up."

"Really? I don't remember hearing about that. Who made the collar?" Bob asked.

"I think that was handled out of Barstow. He hit her in the head with a hammer and made it look like someone robbed that shack of his. The trouble was, she didn't die. She came to and staggered across the lot to us." Earl tossed a couple of frozen burger patties on the grill.

"Yeah, we were fixing a few things, getting ready to open," Susan said as she refilled the carafe with coffee. "I held a wet towel against her head while Earl called the Barstow sheriff. The stupid jerk is rotting in jail right now, and I say good riddance." Susan snorted.

"Huh, I'll have to look that one up. They seldom come all packaged up like that one," Bob said with a chuckle. "If you need us to leave just let us know."

"I don't think so," Earl said as he laid several buns on the grill. "Take a look at this place."

Bob didn't need to take a look. The place was packed. Several customers had made phone calls, passing the word around, and the diner was packed to standing room only. He got up and allowed a young woman holding the hand of a three-year-old and carrying a baby in her arms have his chair. He glanced across the room to where Chase had been seated and he was now inside the kitchen area, helping Susan wait on tables.

"Yeah, people move here thinking it's a nice quiet place to live," a young man in dusty jeans and work boots said. "Then they find out just how quiet it really is."

"I can imagine," Bob said.

A half-hour later Bob had almost decided to return to his car and take a short nap, when Chase set the plates he was carrying on the counter.

"I think we have bingo."

Bob watched a full-sized white van with no lettering and no rear windows pull into the lot and swing around to park next to Cody's Towing. Two men climbed out and the driver popped the hood. "I think you might be right. How do you want to play this?"

"We'll both use the rear door in hopes they don't see us," Chase said as he checked his pistol and dropped it back in the holster. He turned to stare at Marti and Kirk who were still seated.

"You two stay right where you are and get down if they start shooting. We'll let you know what happens."

"She's my daughter, Chase." Marti rose to her feet to glare at him defiantly. "I am not going to sit here when she needs me."

"Chase is right, ma'am," Bob said. "It wouldn't help your daughter any if you got killed in the process."

Chase glanced out the window one more time and Cody had joined the men as they stared at the engine.

"Smooth, real smooth," he whispered before he turned toward the rear door and stared at Bob. "It's really not his first rodeo."

Bob leaned across the table to see out the window. "Yeah, I think you're right. He isn't going to make this easy, is he?"

"No, we need some kind of diversion."

"We can do that," Susan said, as she put two fingers in her mouth and whistled. "Hey, all-y'all, listen up. They need something to draw attention away from them. Now, I just found out the other day that tomorrow's Joe Baxter's birthday, so I think we ought to sing happy birthday to him. Only thing is, he's so old, we'll have to sing it two, maybe three times. Whadda ya say?"

"Now, speak for yourself," Joe said as everyone cheered. Chase slipped quickly through the back door as Susan tried her best to lead the rowdy crowd in the happy birthday song. He hid behind his pickup and struggled to keep from laughing as they slaughtered the music. He'd never heard any crowd at any party stay in tune, but he thought a pack of coyotes might have sung it better tonight. From the corner of his eye, he spied Candy's sleek silhouette against the setting sun for a split second as she skirted behind the barn. He had no idea where Bob and Steve went, but they were both seasoned lawmen and he figured they would be ready when the time came.

Chapter 50

Kyle Boltz leaned over the fender of his big Chevy van and pretended to tinker with the idling engine. Cody came from the interior of his shop to lean over the opposite fender and stared into the engine as well. There wasn't a thing wrong with the van, and that's exactly the way Kyle wanted it. He'd never had to elude the law or make a run for safety, but he wanted a vehicle that would perform like a race car if he ever had to.

"I don't know about this, Kyle," Cody said as he worked the throttle, making the engine race. "There's something going on at the diner. I've never seen so many people there at one time, ever."

"Did you go check it out and see what was happening?"

"No." Cody shook his head.

"Good lord in heaven, Cody. How'd you ever survive this long, if you never check anything out?" Kyle and Jack both laughed at him.

"Well, I didn't want anyone asking questions."

"Asking questions about what? I guess you've got the girls locked up inside the shelter...don't you?"

"Yeah."

"And you've never told anyone they're there, right?"

Cody stared quietly.

"Well, let them ask questions, and if they ask about something you don't want to talk about, tell them you don't know the answer. End of story."

A raucous rendition of Happy Birthday caused them to turn their heads toward the diner. It was followed by two more versions, mingled with tons of laughter.

"Well now, I think that's your answer," Kyle said, slapping Cody on the arm. "You need to relax. "Let's go get the girls. I've got a lot of driving tonight." He slammed the hood on the van and grinned.

Chapter 51

The girls were somber and sat in a tight group except for Abby, who came from the restroom and moved in beside them. The box of salt was quickly passed around as they heard the rattle of keys against the steel door.

"Okay girls" Grace said. "Regardless of what happens, I want you to know I love you. All of you."

"We love you too," Abby said as the rest nodded and hugged one another.

The door swung open and Cody entered, followed by Kyle and Jack. Cody propped the door open with his super-sized wrench and eyed the girls carefully.

"Okay girls. It's moving day. Grab your stuff and let's go. All of you. Now!" There was a difference in Cody's voice that caused several of the girls to look at each other. "Line up. We're all going out at the same time."

Grace took her place at the head of the line, only to have Cody pull her out.

"No, I want you last, to make sure everything goes well. She started to protest, but the look he gave her let her know there would be no discussing the issue at all. She watched as Dianna took the lead. Kyle tried stroking her hair but she brushed his hand aside.

"I see you and I are going to have to get better acquainted," he said with a loud laugh.

Oh God, why is this happening? We prayed and asked you to help us. Then we practiced an attack to get away, not to hurt anyone, but just to get away. And Dianna's a little girl, they all are. She might not know what to do.

Help us. Grace's insides knotted up again as the big man led the way up the stairs. The other girls were following closely in a well-ordered group. It was at the top of the stairs near where the van was parked that Dianna yelled "Hey," causing Kyle to turn around. She threw a handful of salt into his face.

"Ahhh!" he bellowed and swung his right arm in an arch, intending to hit her. Dianna held the piece of clothes hanger up like a threat, but his meaty hand hit her hands, knocking her against the wall. Dianna's heart leaped as he bellowed again and released a truck-load of profanity. The hanger had penetrated his hand completely, and was poking out both sides. She slipped behind him and tried pushing him toward the stairs. Kyle tried to grab her, but she threw her weight into another push, and kept him moving. On the top step of the stairway, she charged once more with a yell of her own. Kyle bellowed as he lost his footing and hit the steps, bounced once and flipped head over heels, landing at Grace's feet.

Jack stared blankly for a few seconds as what had happened soaked into his brain. He started up the stairs to get away but became the recipient of the rest of the salt as the girls threw it into his eyes then ground it in. Cody stood frozen for a couple of seconds before grabbing his wrench and dashing up the stairs, knocking the girls side to side.

He burst into the open to find Chase McGraw waiting.

Chapter 52

Chase stepped back as Cody bellowed and swung the wrench. He instinctively threw up his left arm to block the blow and took the full force of the wrench against his forearm.

"Ahhh!" he yelled as the wrench bit into his arm. Cody charged, swinging the wrench again but Chase was able to duck this one. Buster charged between them with a series of growls and snarls as he circled Cody, biting and tearing at his ankles.

"Yaa! Get away!" Cody yelled, striking at the dog with the wrench. The wrench finally found its mark across Buster's back on the third try, causing the dog to yelp and moved away. Chase charged quickly and kicked Cody in the chest with a side-snap kick, knocking him against the barn. Chase then quickly spun landing a round-house kick to Cody's jaw, knocking him cold.

Chase leaned back against the van, holding his arm. Bob Thornton suddenly appeared from nowhere, shouting orders to Steve and Candy.

"Get those kids out of there and put cuffs on everyone else. Is this Cody?" he asked Chase.

"Yes, that's Cody Waters," Chase said. He pulled his hand away from his arm to see it was covered with blood. The place was suddenly swarming with people, all talking loudly and bragging as to what they had witnessed.

"Excuse me! Excuse me!" Chase could hear Marti as Kirk struggled to open a path so she could see her daughter. She stopped by the van, scanning the crowd. Grace was the last one up the stairs and saw her mother first. She bolted forward to wrap her arms around her and cover her with kisses.

"Oh, I thought I'd lost you forever," Grace repeated time and time again.

"I take it they know each other?" Bob asked Chase with a laugh.

"Yeah, they even look alike." He glanced at Kirk, who had chosen to stand back and watch.

"You'd better get in there and see how she's doing, if you know what's good for you." Kirk looked at him and Chase motioned with his head. "I'm serious. She's going to need your help."

"How's that arm?" Bob asked as he watched the blood dripping from Chase's arm.

"I think it's broken."

"Here, let me see that," Bev said, as she started to roll up his sleeve.

"Ow, careful." Chase pulled away.

"You need a doctor," She turned and yelled. "Hey, Joe, we have an injured man here."

Joe Baxter wove his way through the crowd to where she was standing.

"Oh, yeah, I'd say so. Go fetch my kit from the truck and meet me inside the restaurant."

"You some kind of doctor?" Bob asked as he helped Joe guide Chase through the crowd. They could see Bev waiting on the porch with the medical bag.

"I'm a veterinarian. Joseph Baxter, Doctor of veterinarian medicine. I'm going to stop the bleeding and immobilize your arm. But you need to get to a hospital as soon as possible."

Doctor Baxter seated Chase in a chair and proceeded to cut the sleeve on his shirt. A couple of diners half-drug a groggy Cody into the restaurant and plopped him on a chair. They were followed by Jack who was crying and yelling that the girls had blinded him.

"Shut up, you wussy," Bob said. "You want the whole world to know you got your butt kicked by a bunch of little girls? Why don't you two drag his sorry rear outside and poke his head under the faucet and let it run for a while. But keep an eye on him. I don't trust any of them longer than I can throw them."

Marti entered the diner with all the girls and stood behind Doctor Baxter as he worked on Chase's arm. "Girls, this man is Chase McGraw. He's the one who actually found you. I think you should thank him."

They gathered in a tight circle around Chase and Doctor Baxter. Dianne approached Chase, who was sitting in a chair. She put her arms around his neck as her tears flowed freely.

"Thank you Mr. McGraw. We thought we would never see our friends and families again." She sniffed as she moved away so the others could approach him. Chase was deluged then with hugs, and even a couple of kisses on the cheek.

"Well, that'll have to do until you get to a hospital. The nearest clinic is in Mohave. They're pretty up-to-date on everything because of the military base."

"Can you take a look at Buster for me?" Chase closed his eyes as a pain-wave swept over him.

"What about your dog?"

"Cody hit him with that wrench."

"He did? Well, we'll take him with us and x-ray him at the office. You can give us a call sometime tomorrow when you get up and about." Joe Baxter pulled a card from his shirt pocket and stuffed it into Chase's shirt. "That's my number."

"Hey, one more thing," Chase said as Joe turned to leave.

"Yeah?"

"How are you two related?"

"Me and Bev?"

Chase nodded.

"She's my granddaughter. I'm hoping she'll take over the business someday so I can retire. Why?"

"Just wondering."

"Here," Bev said as she stuffed a small pack of pills into Chase's shirt pocket. "Take one of these if the pain gets unbearable. They are intended for dogs and cats, but you look big and healthy so I figure they are safe enough for you to take. Just make sure you tell the doctor I gave them to you. Now, you sit here and relax while I put your dog into the truck. I'll take good care of him."

Abby came into the diner from the restroom and stopped to stare at Cody Waters. He didn't look like he had moved since being placed in the chair. She shouted several curses and kicked him three times before one of the customers grabbed her.

"Hold on, honey. Leave something for the law to hang," Earl said.

A couple of burly cowboys guided Jack back inside and forced him to sit next to Cody. He was dripping wet and still complaining about being blind. Bob told him to be quiet or he'd let the girls finish the job. Bob then called for an ambulance to transport Kyle, who was unable to walk.

"Sue," Chase said as she walked past the table. "I hate to ask but, I don't know if these girls have eaten. What would it take to feed this crowd?"

"Oh, I'm sure we can work something out. Besides," she raised her cell phone and snapped several pictures of Cody struggling, trying to stand. "They swear Grace cooked them two dinners. But I'll take care of them." She laughed as Cody fell back on his chair.

"What do you plan to do with those?"

"Oh, I don't know. Make a scrap book? That reminds me. Hold still." She took several pictures of him before calling Marti and Grace to pose with him. She finished the set with adding the five girls.

"Okay, listen up folks," Bob Thornton said loudly. "It's starting to get late, and we still have to get to

Bakersfield. We need to divide into groups that we can pack into cars, and we need to decide where we're going."

Chase started feeling nauseous and closed his eyes. He was awakened by someone patting him on the shoulder. He opened his eyes to see Candy's smiling face inches from his own.

"Are you okay enough to ride in a car?"

"Ah, yeah. I think so."

"Good, that'll make it easier. Come on." She took him by his good arm and led him to the front door where her police cruiser was waiting. Chase stopped next to a table where Susan was pouring coffee for Joe Baxter.

"Sue? I guess I'm going to the hospital. Can you please send me a bill for anything these girls might have eaten?"

"Well, I could, but it's all been taken care of."

"Really? How?"

"Don't worry about it. I'll discuss it with you later. Go to the hospital."

"Okay. Can you see that Marti gets these?" He handed her the keys to his truck then let Candy guide him to the cruiser. The tall blond opened the passenger door and helped Chase inside. "I'll take it easy and try to keep you from hurting. Okay?"

Marti glared as the car pulled out of the gravel lot and sped down the highway with its lights flashing. She was surprised the woman hadn't turned on the siren.

"It's been a rough day, officer. Can't we all give our testimony tomorrow?" Grace asked.

"There are some things that are better if they're done while everything's fresh."

"Yes, but we're emotionally drained, and I was hoping to spend time with my daughter," Marti said. "She also would like to see her son."

"Yes, I know but…" He stopped and looked around at the girls.

"Okay, I'm going to make a deal with you all. I need a bunch of you to take us around to where you were locked up, show us anything you might think of interest, and then I'll let you go. But, I'll need every one of you in my office in the morning. Okay?"

"Yeah, sure." Several of the girls nodded.

"This is very important that you do exactly what I say. Because if you don't, Cody Waters and his friends might all go free. Now, I don't think any of you would want that. Would you? It's important you all come to my office in the morning."

Marti followed the small crowd to the bomb shelter and stood near the door as the girls told their stories. It took Grace three tries before she could re-enter the shelter. The part that caused Marti's stomach to churn was the fact that several of them, excluding Grace and the twelve-year-old and Dianna, had been living on the streets and selling themselves when they were kidnapped.

Finally, Officer Thornton followed them back to where the cars were parked and took their pledge to show up in his office at ten 'o-clock in the morning. Marti watched while Kirk loaded several girls into his car before asking what he was doing.

"I'm going to take them to Bakersfield so they can be in court in the morning. Don't worry," he added as she gave him a quizzical look. "I've made a reservation for separate rooms at Motel 6."

"Okay, I've got room for three more in the truck." Dianna and Grace both climbed in; followed by one of the girls Marti wasn't familiar with, leaving room for Chase when they got to Mohave.

A half-hour later, Marti idled Chase's truck into the patient pick-up zone at the medical clinic. Officer Candy Martin had pulled her car to the curb and they were getting ready to load Chase into her car. She double parked and stepped out of the truck.

"Excuse me, I can take him to his house," she said.

"I'm just following orders, ma'am."

"Yes, I know you are. But I have to go there anyway, and I've got several of the girls already." The passenger doors opened and the girls waved at her. "I mean, you can take him, but since I've got to go to his house anyway, I might as well be the one who takes him."

"If you're sure it's alright."

"Believe me, it alright."

"Okay, let me move the squad car."

They moved a heavily sedated Chase into the backseat of the pickup when Officer Candy cautioned them to be careful. "The arm was broken so go easy with it. He's medicated pretty heavily, so I doubt he'll wake up until you get him home. Oh, and thank you for doing this. It will give me a chance to see my daughter before she goes to bed."

"You're welcome," Marti said with a big smile, but she felt like dirt inside. She had no idea why she felt jealous of Officer Candy with her long, sleek body, golden hair and blue eyes. She really didn't have any ties on Chase McGraw in the first place.

Marti did notice that the sheriff's car followed her to the Bakersfield city limits before it turned off. Marti drove slowly through town and turned toward the ranch. After what felt like an eternity, she parked the truck next to her car. Janice came from the house with Walter Rogers in tow as nearly everyone climbed out of the truck, except Chase and Dianna. Chase had fallen asleep and flopped over to lie against Dianna, who seemed to be enjoying the attention. The girl looked up at Marti and gave a tentative smile, holding her fingers against her healing lips.

"I'm sorry you had to ride all the way home like that. Let us get him off you."

"Well, I didn't mind it at all. Besides, I haven't been back to the place I grew up in a long while."

"And where did you grow up?"

"A Texas cattle ranch outside of Austin. This looks kind of like it."

Chapter 53

Chase woke to the smell of bacon and coffee, mingled with laughter. He started to roll out of bed but a bolt of pain in his arm caused him to roll back the other way with a loud moan. He thought about lying there until his arm was completely healed, but he also knew that was impossible. The bathroom was calling him at the moment, but the problem was getting out of bed without disturbing his left arm. He finally managed to slide his feet to the floor without using his arm. By the time he had shaved and brushed his teeth, Janice was knocking on the door.

"Hey Chase, are you alive?"

"Yeah, barely. I'll be out there once I figure out how to get dressed."

"You need some help? I can give you a hand."

"No, don't you dare." Chase sat on the edge of the bed, studying the jeans in his right hand.

"Why not? I'm your big sister. Besides," he heard her giggle, "how do you think you got into your pajamas last night?"

"I can help him get dressed."

He wasn't sure, but he thought the voice belonged to Dianna. He suddenly remembered snippets of the drive home. Either it was part of a dream, or Dianna had kissed him on the cheek, not once but twice.

"No, I'll send Walt to help him as soon as he gets back from the hen house. He's a marvel with cattle, but not too much with chickens."

He finally worked the jeans on, inch by inch, but couldn't figure out how to button them up.

"There you are," Janice said with a chuckle as Walt came through the door.

"You'd better find someone else to herd your chickens, 'cause me and that brood don't get along too well," Walt said with a snort. "It took me that long to get a dozen eggs."

Chase tried again to button his pants before flopping backwards on the bed. He was about ten seconds from calling Janice to come button them when he remembered something from their past. He had seen Janice once, when they were both teenagers, lay on her back to button a new pair of jeans. He lay back on the bed, said a prayer for buttoning pants with one hand and got it done on the third try. He walked to the kitchen carrying his boots in his right hand. Dianna saw him and jumped up, offering him her chair.

"No, that's your chair. Sit back down."

"And I gave it to you. Sit down and I'll help you with your boots." True to her word, she sat on the floor facing Chase and worked both boots on snuggly.

Matthew staggered into the kitchen rubbing his eyes and headed straight toward Chase with a grin. He stopped and stared at the cast on Chase's left arm.

"That's okay, honey," Marti said. "Chase has a big owie, and the doctor put that on there to help make it better."

Matthew touched the cast with his fingers before leaning to kiss it. Then he smiled and crawled into Chase's lap.

"Come here, baby," Grace said with a chuckle. "Let's change your diaper before you get everyone all wet."

"Okay, breakfast is ready," Janice announced. "Better dig in. You've got to see Bob Thornton pretty soon."

"Why?" Dianna paused in the middle of spooning scrambled eggs, bacon and fried potatoes onto a plate.

"We're the ones who were stuck inside that bomb shelter…not him."

"But he's the one who's collecting the information for the District Attorney to put those guys in prison."

Chase gave her a big grin.

"Oh, okay then. Here, I got it for you." She slid the plate in front of Chase and started another for herself.

The kitchen suddenly got quieter as they ate. Chase was sipping a second cup of coffee while Dianna was moving her food around on her plate.

"What's the matter, honey? Don't you like your breakfast," Janice asked.

"Oh, the food's good." She smiled and took another bite.

"Then what's wrong? You're acting like something's wrong," Chase asked.

"No, nothing's wrong," she said with a shrug. "I couldn't sleep last night, so I snuck out and looked around. This is a beautiful ranch. Really nice."

"Thank you. I try to keep it that way," Janice said. "You said you grew up on a ranch in Texas, didn't you? Was it a happy time for you?"

"Yeah. I lived with my grandparents until they died. Their daughter was my mom, but she died of cancer. My grandpa and grandma died when a tanker ran a stop sign."

"I'm sorry," Chase said. "Why aren't you home on the ranch?"

"Their youngest son, my uncle Jimmy, couldn't keep his hands off me so I ran away. I came to California, the land of milk and honey." She shrugged and sipped her coffee. She stared at Chase with watery eyes. "Can I ask you a question?"

Chase set his cup on the table and stared back. "Ask away."

"Will you be my daddy?"

"What?"

"Will you be my daddy? I've never really had one. I remember my momma, but she's gone. Yesterday was the best time I've ever had in my life. I've never had a daddy. Will you be mine?"

Chase was dumbstruck, but then thought it might be a joke. Before he could speak, she suddenly jumped up from the table.

"It's okay, I understand. It was a stupid question anyway."

"No!" Chase grabbed her arm and pulled her toward him. "It's not a stupid question." He rose from the table and gave her a sideways hug. "You just took me by surprise. That's a lot to think about. Besides, the court might have a problem with it, me being single and you being fifteen. But I'll see about getting temporary custody for as long as this court case takes, then we'll see what happens. But if it makes you feel better you can call me your dad."

Chase looked at Janice. "How about it, Aunt Janice? Can she use one of the spare rooms until I can rent a house or apartment someplace?"

"I'm already working on the problem, and you don't have to rent a house somewhere else." She smiled as she carried the empty plates to the sink. "You're always welcome here."

Dianna broke free from Chase's one-armed hug. I'd better get ready," she said and scampered down the hallway. Janice paused before setting the plates on the counter. "You'd better get to Bob's office before he comes hunting you. And…" she said as he started to turn away "You'd better stop on your way home at someplace that sells women's clothing. If you haven't noticed Papa, your daughter's wearing the same clothes she had on last night, and I didn't see any baggage. I'll bet she doesn't even have a tooth brush."

Chapter 54

Chase and Dianna stopped at the local Tractor Supply on their way home from the Sheriff's Department. It was probably more by habit than anything else, seeing as the Tractor Supply was where he bought most of his own jeans, shirts and hats. It didn't dawn on him that Dianna would need something to wear under the new clothes she was going to buy. That would require another store altogether, a store he would not normally go inside on his own. Dianna spent the first half hour looking at the shirts hanging in the racks and comparing prices. He finally texted Janice and asked for a list of things a girl might need, then pulled Dianna aside to grin at her.

"Hey, rule number one. You don't have to look at the prices. Okay? I'm buying these clothes for you, whether or not the court says you get to stay with us. They are going to be yours. So, pick out several shirts and pants so we can go somewhere else and get your personal stuff."

Armed with several bags of clothes and a pair of cowgirl boots and hat, they drove across the parking lot toward Target, hoping they might have most of the things she still needed.

Dianna started comparing prices a second time and he decided it was better if he stayed next to her and helped her choose. Hairspray, a good tooth brush, toothpaste, deodorant, dental floss and a female razor. Chase grinned at the pile of stuff inside the shopping cart. He couldn't remember ever buying any of these things, even when he was married. Next came women's tampons and underwear.

"You don't have to stay here for this, Pops, unless you really want to."

Chase stared at her for a couple of seconds. She was standing by the cart holding a plastic bag of panties.

"Are those the right size?"

"Yes, I think so." She eyeballed the bag.

"Then get several more bags, unless you want to be doing laundry every few days. Do the same for your bras. I guess you need those too."

"Yes, I'm not very big, but I do need a bra." Her face reddened as she ambled toward the rack containing bras.

"Okay," Chase said, checking Janice's shopping list on his phone. "I think we've got just about everything we need. Do you want to double-check the list?"

Dianna took the phone and quickly compared the list to the shopping cart.

"I think it's okay."

"Well, then let's go home and eat. I'm starving. Oh, one more thing," Chase said as they passed a rack of books. He grabbed a Bible from the end cap.

"A Bible?"

"Yep, a Bible. Everybody needs a good Bible." He smiled at her as they waited in line. "Didn't you ever have a Bible of your own?"

"Just one of those New Testaments they handed out at school a few years ago. I guess they don't do that now."

"No, you're right. They don't hand those out in schools anymore. I wish they did. Anyway, read something out of that every day. Janice and I will help you if you need a hand."

Chase started the truck and pulled into traffic behind an Amazon Prime delivery truck. Dianna sat staring quietly out the spotty windshield. They had gone about a half a mile before she broke her silence.

"Why did you do this?"

"Do what?"

"Buy me all that stuff. You spent a lot of money on me." She eyed him through misty eyes.

"Oh," Chase nodded. "I bought you the clothes because you needed them, mostly. You didn't have anything to change into, and Janice told me to take you shopping on the way home. Besides," he looked at her and grinned, "I don't want my daughter to look like a street urchin...Why?" he added after a minute.

"Why? Most guys want something in return when they get you something."

Chase signaled and glanced over his shoulder as he changed lanes.

"Well," he released a deep breath, "I'll make you this promise right now, Dianna Rigsby, whenever I buy you clothes or food or anything else, it's because I love you, and I don't expect anything from you. That's the bottom line."

They rode in silence a few more miles before Chase turned off the highway toward the ranch. That's when he noticed Dianna's tear-streaked face and pulled over to park off the roadway.

"Hey, what's the matter? Did I do something wrong?"

"No. No one's ever bought me new clothes. I usually wear hand-me-downs. And no one's ever said they love me without wanting something in return. Oh, I hope to God you really do."

Chase put the truck into park and unfastened his seatbelt. He gave her a hug then scooted back to his spot to study her a minute.

"Maybe no one you've lived with has been a Christian. I don't know. All I know is, I love you as if you are my own daughter and I'll never hurt you on purpose. Do you believe that?

"Yes...I guess so."

"That's not good enough. We've got to get that to a real honest-to-goodness 'for sure.' Can you do that?" He laughed as she nodded. That was good enough for now.

Chapter 55

Grace sat on the sofa in Janice's family room sipping a cup of hot tea. Several of the girls, especially the very young ones, had already gone home with their parents with the promise they would be back in court for the arraignment, which promised to be a long one, followed by a longer wait for the trial. It was something she was not looking forward to. She was also positive that no matter what the outcome of the hearings and the trial, there would be some people who would be convinced that she had been sleeping with the men on trial. While the thought still bothered her, she had come to realize that her feelings had their base in her pride and wouldn't matter one way or the other down the road. What did matter was the girls' safety.

Dianna was crawling around on the floor teaching Matthew how to roll a plastic car Chase had given him. Grace grinned as she watched the little game her mother and Chase McGraw were playing with each other, which at the moment was more interesting than Matthew's plastic car. Chase was punching letters into his cell phone as he watched Marti from across the room. It was like he was on some sort of stakeout until Marti turned toward him and he quickly diverted his attention back to his cell phone.

Her mother, on the other hand, suddenly became extremely conscious of her hair, and felt a need to brush back unruly strands every few seconds and giggle like a teenager. She also seemed to check with him frequently to see if he needed refills of ice tea, or a helping of chips and salsa.

You sly old fox Grace thought to herself. *There's a whole lot more going on than my rescue.* Yes, Chase McGraw was an excellent investigator who knew what to do and when to do it. But he also had the rugged look of an American cowboy that most women found appealing.

A timer went off and Chase excused himself in order to remove a couple of tri-tips from the grill. Marti quickly found a reason to cross the room to where she could see Chase through the window as he placed a pack of hot-links on the grill. It was Janice's 39th birthday and Chase and Walt had decided to go all out. They had purchased a large container of potato salad, garlic bread, chili beans and ice cream from the deli. Glancing at the table, they had bought enough food for several days. Marti quickly turned and walked back to check on the table setting as Chase came back inside a second later.

"I'll be slicing the meat in a few minutes, so everybody can start getting ready."

"Finally," Janice said and laid aside the copy of Ranch Life and got to her feet. The men had ordered her not to work on her birthday, because they would handle everything. From the expression on Janice's face, Grace could see the order was tearing her apart, and the best present they could give her was to let her be in charge of the kitchen.

Chase's cell phone chimed and he stepped aside to answer the text. Walt took over cutting the try-tip after Chase grumbled while he typed into the phone. The expression on Chase's face changed into horror as he stared at the phone.

"No! You can't do this to me! Agh," he yelled and threw the phone across the room where it bounced off the recliner three feet from where Dianna was. She grabbed the phone and began playing with the keys.

"What's it doing, Pops?"

"It died, that's what it's doing. The stupid thing's been acting up but I kept getting distracted and didn't buy a replacement. Now, it just went blank in the middle of texting Bob, who needs what I was sending to use in court." He glared at the phone and shouted "I hate you."

"Calm down, Pops. I've got it," Dianna said as she punched numbers, paused, then punched some more. She waited a few seconds then handed Chase the phone.

"There you go. Finish your text."

"How'd you do that?" Chase said, starring at the phone.

"I just reset the phone. You've picked up a bug someplace. I'll try removing it sometime this afternoon."

Dianna scooped Matthew into her arms and put him in the highchair with the car. "How about some tri-tip, big guy?"

Chase punched away on the phone for a couple of minutes before turning to give Dianna a hug.

"Maybe I should take you on all my cases to man the phone and computer."

"I'd go, if I got to carry a gun." She looked up at him with a crooked grin as she cut a piece of tri-tip into tiny pieces for Matthew.

The meal went as Chase and Walt had wanted. The food was excellent and everyone was almost too full to enjoy the chocolate birthday cake topped with strawberries and vanilla ice cream. Chase gave his sister a new pair of silver spurs and Walt bought her a new hat. But Janice's most treasured gift by far was a framed picture of tiny hand prints signed to Aunt Janice from Matthew.

******

They were about halfway home waiting for a light to change when Grace grinned at her mother.

"So, tell me how long has it been going on?"

"Tell you what's been going on? I don't follow you."

"You and Chase."

"What about me and Chase? What are you talking about?"

The light changed and Grace nudged the gas pedal.

"I was watching the both of you tonight, and both of you were playing this little game with each other. You would watch his every move until he looked at you, and he would do the same thing. You probably didn't see it, but you definitely have an admirer.

"No, I don't know what you were looking at, but Chase and I are nothing but friends."

"Mama," Grace laughed as she turned left. "You've always taught me to tell the truth, even when I was a little girl."

"I am telling the truth. I don't know what you were looking at."

"I will bet you anything I have that Janice will tell you the same thing if you call her tomorrow. And, there's nothing wrong with you having a crush on Chase McGraw."

"I'm telling you, I don't have a crush on Chase."

Grace pulled her car into the driveway and killed the engine. She studied her mother for a few seconds as a dog barked somewhere in the distance.

"It really is okay with me, Mama. If I was a little bit older, or he was a little bit younger, I'd be after him myself. That is, unless you really don't want him, then I just might move in and…"

"Okay, your point is well taken," Marti said quietly. "I really didn't think it showed. Was I that obvious? "

"You both were kind of cute."

"I really did make an ass out of myself, didn't I?" Marti looked away and sniffed.

"No, you didn't. I'd tell you if you did. I was just trying to discover how much you love him," Grace said, laying a hand on Marti's arm. "And it wouldn't offend me in the least if you did start dating someone and fell in love and got remarried."

"Really?"

"Yes, really. I made up my mind to do the same thing while I was being locked inside that bomb shelter. I am not going to sit about feeling sorry for myself. We're both young and we have a lot of love to give to someone. Now," she undid her seatbelt, "I guess I'd better put Matthew to bed."

Marti release her belt and opened the door.

"You're right, of course. I didn't want to admit it, but I've had a crush on Chase for several weeks now. And I've never forgotten the kiss he gave me."

"He kissed you?"

"Yes."

"On the lips?"

"Of course, on the lips."

Grace unbuckled her son and held him to her breast as she closed the door with her foot.

"Did you kiss him back?"

"Yes, I did kiss him back. And I'd do it again, if I could."

"Wow!" Grace said softly. "I guess I might be getting a new dad sooner than I thought."

"But, he's never given me any indication that he feels the same way about me," Marti said as she unlocked the front door to the house.

"Did he kiss you first?"

Marti turned on the lights and held the door open for Grace and Matthew.

"Yes, I was crying because we couldn't find you and…"

"He does." Grace said, cutting her off.

"He does what?"

"Feel the same way about you." Grace gave her a grin. "All you have to do is find out how much you love each other."

Chapter 56

"Well, that's the best we've gotten from him." Bob poured two cups of black coffee and made a face when he tasted it. Chase set his cup on top of a file cabinet.

"He isn't talking?"

Bob shook his head. "His lips are welded tight. Not a peep, no matter if I'm nice or threatening to kill him. Nothing."

Chase looked up as a police woman brought Dianna and two of the girls into the room from giving their depositions.

"How'd they do?" Chase asked.

"They did great, *Daddy*. They did real good."

"Daddy? What am I missing here?" Bob said.

"Dianna said Chase is going to adopt her."

"That right? Are you going to adopt her?"

"I told her I would think about it."

"Good luck. They're all wards of the court until we talk to their parents, and I've got Sarah working on that right now. I still haven't figured out how she's going to find yours, since you haven't given us any address or phone number." He glared at Dianna.

She shrugged as she lifted the coffee pot and started looking for a cup. "That's because I don't have one. They're my foster parents and are always on the move and changing their cell phone numbers. They collect the checks from a post office box."

"Here, take mine. I haven't drunk out of it." Chase handed her his cup. She took a sip and made a face at Bob.

"What are you trying to do, kill everyone?" She dumped the coffee and started washing the pot.

They both looked up as Marti and Grace entered the room. "How'd it go?" Chase asked.

"We both got chewed out royally from the doctor on duty," Grace said. "He said we should have gone to the hospital the minute we got back to Bakersfield."

"He's right. You should have," Bob said.

"Yeah, but it was getting very late, and Chase was passed out in the back seat of his truck. Anyway," she continued as Dianna turned the coffeemaker on. "I'm fine. Cody Waters actually acted like a gentleman and he never tried to molest me, not once."

"No beatings or rope burns from being tied up?"

"Nope, not a one. Dianna had been beaten up before she arrived."

"How about food? Were you every hungry or feeling starved?"

"No. I got fed three times a day. It wasn't the kind of food I would normally eat. It was more like man-food; I gained five pounds, but I was never hungry."

"Well, he's not giving us much to go on," Chase said with a chuckle. Maybe I should have taken another hit for the cause."

"Who whacked you?" Bob asked Dianna as she washed the coffee mugs.

"Kyle. I don't know if it's his real name. He was just some big creep who grabbed me off the street into the back of a van. He hit me three or four times I think, when I put up a fight."

"Would you know him if you saw him again?"

"Oh yeah," she said with a nod. "It'll be real easy to spot him. I left some trail-marks." She bent her fingers like claws to show her fingernails. And I'm the one who pushed him down the stairs."

"Could you pick him out of a line-up?"

"Sure, if you think it would help."

Bob took a sip of fresh coffee and grinned. "Yes, most anything is going to help at this point. And this is a great cup of coffee." He pushed a button on the telephone and waited for the ring.

"Sarah? Make an appointment for Dianna to get checked out at the hospital. Yes, again. I want to know what kind of injuries she got. Yes. You know, hangnails, anything. Thanks."

He took another sip of coffee. "In the meantime, we have to figure out what Cody Waters knows about this operation."

"Let me talk to him," Grace said quietly.

"No, I don't think that's advisable," Bob said, shaking his head. "You're the one he grabbed and there might be some sort of feelings or something. It could get messy."

"I don't think so. I got the feeling that he really liked me for some reason. Maybe he was hoping I would like him too."

"It's not a bad idea, Bob," Chase said. "If she went in alone, she might be able to talk some sense into him."

"You can watch through that window you've got in the wall, and if it gets too bad, you can pull me out."

"Okay, but I'm pulling you the instant it looks like he's losing it."

"Just be his friend," Chase said thoughtfully, "especially at first. Then try to find out the names of the big bosses and where they're shipping the girls. Bob and his men can take it from there."

******

Grace entered the interrogation room by herself and stood watching Cody for a few seconds. He was seated in a straight-back chair fidgeting and tapping his foot.

"May I sit down, Cody?"

He looked up and shrugged. "Did they get desperate and send you in to question me?"

"No, I asked to see you."

He looked up and snorted. "Why would you do that?"

"I saw the way they were treating you and didn't like it. I thought you might like a friend."

"That all sounds nice, but you didn't like me very much the night I got arrested." He sat up straight in the chair to glare at her.

A grin slowly crept across Chase's lips as he watched Grace reached across the table and pat the back of Cody's wrist.

"No, you've got that wrong, Cody. I didn't like being locked up, that's for sure. But I always found you pleasant to talk to. I would have liked you more if you would have set me free."

"I told you I couldn't do that."

"I know what you said, but I wouldn't have told the police right away. You would have had time to get away."

They sat staring at one another for a long minute before Cody snorted. "Well, it doesn't really matter anymore, does it?"

"What doesn't matter?"

"You, me. Me letting you go. None of that matters now.

"Probably not. Although Deputy Thornton said he could go easy on you if you helped him."

"Really?" Cody said with a high-pitched laugh. "Do you know what those men will do if I try to help? I'll become coyote bait. You can tell him no thanks."

She tried for several more minutes without drawing any response from him at all. Finally, she got up from the table and patted his manacled hands.

"I'll come back later, when you feel like talking. Bye, Cody Waters."

Cody waited until she was out of the room.

"Bye, Grace Peterson."

Chapter 57

Chase answered his cell phone on the third ring. "Hello?"

"Mr. McGraw? This is Beverly Baxter. Buster says he's ready to come home."

"He is?" Chase chuckled and set his coffee cup down on the desk.

"Yes, he is definitely ready."

"And I suppose he told you he was ready."

"Well, yeah, if you can understand Border Collie," Beverly laughed. "Nothing was broken, but he is bruised and tender. You'll have to hold him back from some of his normal activities because he's an active dog and gets around pretty well for his age and after being injured."

"Okay, when would you like me to get him?"

"Any time. Just let me know so one of us will be here."

"How about now? I can be there by noon."

"That would be fine. We'll look forward to seeing you."

"Dianna?" He raised his voice to be heard in the next room.

"Yeah, Dad?" She poked her head through the opened door.

"Want to take a ride with me? That was the vet on the phone and Buster's ready to come home."

"Sure; give me ten minutes to get ready."

He chuckled as she half skipped down the hall to her room. He went out back where Janice was giving Marti and

Grace riding lessons. Janice was holding Matthew on the saddle in front of her. He watched them a couple of minutes before walking out to where they were.

"Excuse me, Grace, but I'd like to borrow your son for a couple of hours, if it's okay."

"Sure, I guess so. What for?"

"The vet called and Buster's ready to come home. I'm taking Dianna with me."

"Oh, that will be fun for him. Give me a few minutes and I'll make sure he has everything in his diaper bag."

"Well, I'm sure Dianna will keep you men in line," Janice said with a crooked grin. "Have fun."

"We will." He turned to leave then looked back as Marti spoke.

"You take care of my grandson, Chase McGraw."

"I will. I'm going to get the car seat out of your car if that's okay."

He bumped into the half-closed gate and side-stepped around it as Dianna bounded out the back door. Chase looked at her and pointed as he walked toward Marti's car.

"I'm going to get the car seat. We're taking Matt with us."

"Oh, I thought you wanted my company. What you really want is for me to babysit Matt while you get your dog." She stopped in the graveled driveway with her hands on her hips and glared at him.

"No," Chase said as he unsnapped the seat. "I asked you because I wanted your company and I thought you'd like the ride. Then, I saw Matt and decided to take him too. You don't have to go."

"I know that, you knot-head." She shook her head and laughed. "You have to learn when I'm teasing, Pops."

Chase couldn't remember half of what they discussed on the ride to Joseph Baxter's veterinary office, other than that her views on life were fairly conservative, or she was putting on a heck of a performance. He had to wake

Matthew when he parked the truck. He took the time to change Matthew's diaper before entering the office. Beverly had Buster running free in the office and one look at Matthew caused a barking fit. Chase put Matthew on the floor and they resumed their game of *Catch Me If You Can.*

"I take it they missed each other," Beverly said.

"I thought they might entertain each other on the ride home." He gave her his credit card.

"Well, catch me up on things. What happened to the three guys that kidnapped the girls?"

Dianna looked at Chase and waited until he nodded. "It's okay. You won't be able to tell her anything that they can't get from the papers."

Chase paid Buster's bill while Dianna told her everything that had been going on. Buster leaped into the back seat when he opened the door, causing Chase to cringe. That dog was trying to waste everything Doctor Baxter had done. They were on their way home when Chase pulled into line at the local McDonalds and asked Dianna what she wanted.

"A fresh garden salad with ranch dressing."

He stared at her for a few seconds. "A what?"

"A garden salad with ranch dressing? That's what I want," she added as Chase studied her like she was crazy.

"Okay. a fresh garden salad with ranch dressing, two Happy Meals, and a number three with cheese," he said to the squawk box.

They sat in the parking lot eating their lunch. He thought Dianna was going to die laughing as he unwrapped one of the Happy Meals and fed it to Buster. "Well, he gets hungry once in a while,"

"I don't care if you feed him a Happy Meal," Dianna said. "That's just the first time I've seen anyone give one to a dog." They ate in silence for a few minutes. Chase wiped his lips and fingers and cleared his throat.

"I asked you to come so I could tell you something that's been on my mind."

Dianna stared at him with misty eyes. "You've decided you don't want me."

"No! Just the opposite. You've been with us several days and you keep your room clean and do your own laundry. You don't argue and work hard and try to be pleasant. I've really grown fond of you these past few days, and I'm happy to call you my daughter."

"Oh, thank you, thank you," she said hugging him.

"Now, that doesn't mean you can trash your room. You understand that, don't you?"

"Don't worry about that," she said with a laugh. "I like my room clean."

Dianna tossed their trash into a can while Buster found a spot in the rear seat where he could comfortably see Matthew. Both Matthew and Buster had their eyes closed by the time Chase pulled onto the highway. A dam seemed to crumble inside Dianna as she told him about her life and the foster homes she had been in, followed by a brief stint on the streets. Chase listened without saying much. It was later inside his room that his own heart broke as he knelt in prayer.

"Forgive me, Lord. Not for the petty sins I continually fall into. But forgive me for who I am. I've seen kids like Dianna all my life, but I haven't really seen them. I haven't tried to understand or love them. I stepped around them and ignored them. I'm sorry.

Chapter 58

"So, what's happened?" Chase said as he watched Kyle through the two-way mirror. The man really looked beat up. His right eye was swollen and discolored, and was sporting several stitches from being banged against the stairs. His left knee was wrapped in a blue leg brace, and his right hand was bandaged from being skewered with the clothes hanger. What held Chase's attention was the way the man was seated at the table, looking cocky and confident as if he held some sort of secret.

"Still not talking?"

"No, his lips are glued shut," Bob said in disgust. "Sometimes I wish we could go back to the old way where you could beat a confession out of a slime ball like him."

"Well, let's just see if we can figure out what his secret is."

"How do you propose to do that?"

"By using our secret weapon."

Chase walked briskly toward Sarah's office. He opened the door without knocking and found Dianna standing on a chair as she slipped several files into a cabinet. Sarah glanced up from her computer screen but continued typing.

"Yes, what do you need now, Chase?"

"Well, is that any way to talk to the guy who's buying lunch today?"

"Okay, sorry." She quit typing to look up at him. "Keeping in mind you no longer work here, what do you need me to do?"

"Actually, nothing. I just need to borrow Dianna for a while." Chase leaned against the doorpost and halfway folded his arms. He gave Sarah a crooked grin that caused her stomach to flutter.

"You know, Chase McGraw, there are sometimes I really hate you."

"Why, what did I do?"

"Nothing," Sarah said as Dianna jumped off the chair and wiped her hands on her pant legs. "And that's the trouble. You always come trotting down the hall and ask me to do some of the almost impossible things then give me that stupid little grin, and sure enough, I'll end up doing them. Then," Sarah turned toward Dianna, "all I ever got from him was that grin. No thank you, not even a 'you're an angel, Sarah'." She turned back to Chase. "Go on, take your daughter and get out of here."

"I wonder what's got her goat today?" Chase mumbled as he guided Dianna back down the hall to the interrogation room.

"You don't know?" Dianna asked with giggle.

"Know what?"

"Why she was acting that way."

Chase stopped with his hand on the doorknob to look at her.

"No, I've always thought that she just had some bad mood swings when she got like that." He held the door open for her.

"No," Dianna shook her head and laughed loudly. "She gets that way because she's in love with you."

"Nah." Chase shook his head as he led her to a table holding several bags of evidence. "Besides, she's married and has a couple of kids."

"It doesn't matter. She still is."

"Who is still what?" Bob asked as they sat down.

"Sara's in love with my dad."

"Yeah? Well everyone knows that." Bob snorted.

"No she's not." Chase cocked his head to one side. "We're just friends."

"You might be friends, but she's in love with you. She always has been, from the first day you arrived out of the Academy. Now," he leaned back to study Chase, "what do we need her for?"

"For this." Chase reached inside one of the bags and retrieved Kyle's cell phone.

"We've already had forensics go through all that stuff, and they didn't find much. That phone's encrypted."

"Yes, but some kids seem to find a way of doing stuff with their cell phones and computers that we adults don't comprehend." He handed the phone to Dianna and grinned. "Do you want to see what you can do with this?"

"Sure." She took the phone and began punching numbers.

"You know, we don't really have to know everything on that phone to develop a good case, especially if he thinks we've broken into his private stuff. A couple of names and numbers, a few texts…we might even be able to get a few of his acquaintances to run or flip and become witnesses to save their own hides."

"Bingo!" Dianna yelled.

"Bingo? Whadda ya got?" Bob and Chase both looked over her shoulders.

"I'm into his secured account."

"And what does that mean?" Chase asked.

"What that means is, he's been running two accounts on the same phone. It's like having two separate phones inside one case. One of them acts like a regular telephone that anyone can see and use. The second account is on the cloud and hidden, and no one but the owner is supposed to see or use it, or even know it's there. But here it is." She slid the phone for them both to see.

"Wow! Bingo is right." Chase pulled a notepad and pen from his pocket to copy names and phone numbers.

"What I don't understand is how did you know about a hidden account and find it so fast." Bob plopped back into his chair and stared at Chase as he scribbled away. "I've had several of the best cybercrimes detectives look at that phone, and they came up empty-handed."

"I read about it in a tech magazine a few months ago and thought I'd check it out and see if this phone had one, and it does" Dianna said. "Whose phone is it, anyway?"

"Your friend Kyle's," Bob said.

"Well, if it helps put him away, let me go completely through it. I'll bet I can find some real juicy stuff for you." She giggled and shook her head. "You're supposed to build an encrypted password, but the jerk is so full of himself, he used *studmuffin23*. Not too bright, if you ask me."

******

Bob had Sarah contact the cyber-crimes unit and had them come to the interrogation room so they could watch Dianna work her magic on Kyle's phone. They sat and took notes, then asked Bob if they could borrow her every now and then to search for hidden accounts or empty folders that weren't really empty.

Chase seated himself at the table in the interrogation room and waited until they brought Kyle back inside.

"Oh, so they thought they'd bring the big guns in to see if I'd crack." He laughed and reached for a cigarette.

"Sorry, this is a no-smoking area."

"So, what are you going to do, arrest me?"

"No, I don't have to. There's a whole room full of cops right behind that mirror, waiting to haul your carcass off. So, I'd recommend that you put that away and listen for a few minutes, because what I'm about to say will probably change your life forever."

"Fire away." He leaned back in his chair and smirked. "You've got nothing on me. I heard about those girls and was just going to load them inside my van and take

193

them to the nearest police station and let 'em go. It was that stupid _____ that threw salt into my eyes and stabbed me with a clothes hanger.

"Think so?" Chase said with a laugh. "The same fifteen-year-old girl you beat up?"

"Yeah, the same girl. When we get to court, it's my word against hers. I'll eat her alive."

"Okay," Chase looked Kyle up and down, "let's quit playing games. First of all, that girl? Dianna? Who you referred to as a _____ ?" She's my daughter."

"Daughter?"

"Yes, you snatched my daughter off the street, and I know she's not lying. Second, that piece of clothes hanger? You're lucky she stabbed your hand, instead of skewering you like a hog.

"But most of all," Chase pulled his notepad from his shirt pocket and began reading names, telephone numbers and credit card numbers of high profile business men, a few politicians and at least one judge. The blood drained from Kyle's face as he listened. Chase read for several minutes before flipping his notepad closed and putting it back into his pocket. He stood looking down at the man.

"Now, that's just the beginning. You're going to be locked away for a very, very long time Kyle, and I can't say I'm sorry. So, if you want to see if the D.A. might be merciful and cut a couple of years off what you're being charged with, have at it. Frankly, I hope he doesn't. I don't want to ever see your face on the street again."

"Wait, wait," Kyle choked out as Chase reached for the doorknob.

"Yeah, whadda ya want, Kyle? You ready to cut some sort of deal? Want me to send in Bob Thornton?"

"Yeah, I'll talk. Really."

"Okay, sit tight."

******

Chase returned with four polish sandwiches and four helpings of french fries. He found Bob sitting and watching Kyle Boltz talk to a man and a woman from the District Attorney's office.

"Thanks," Bob said as Chase handed him his sandwich. He set his own sandwich and fries on the table and passed the paper bag to Dianna.

"Thanks, Pop. I'm going to have lunch with Sarah, if that's okay."

"Sure. Have fun."

"I'll bet Sarah loves having her in her office," Bob said. "It'll be the first time the filing's been done since we hired her."

Chase took a big bite and watched Kyle in an animated moment as he waved his arms around.

"When do you think he'll run out of steam?"

"Heck if I know. Maybe never." Bob retrieved Kyle's phone from the evidence bag and punched some numbers. "Your daughter found this, then quickly quit working with it. She said it was making her sick." He punched one more number and passed the phone to Chase.

"Take a look at this."

"Oh, my Lord," Chase said as a video of a judge he knew was having sex with a child. He quickly passed the phone back to Bob.

"Man, you can certainly ruin a good lunch."

"I didn't ruin your lunch. He did," Bob said pointing at the phone.

"Why would anyone, let alone a judge, let someone video them doing something like that?" Chase said, shaking his head.

"Maybe he didn't know he was being filmed."

"Blackmail?"

"Maybe. We have to look at all the angles. And," Bob pointed toward the phone, "I do know Harry's handed down a couple of really strange rulings lately."

"Well, it looks as though it's over," Chase said as a couple of guards escorted Kyle from the room. The two deputies compared notes and left the room a few minutes later.

They both ate in silence for a few minutes before Chase tossed his empty fry container in the trash.

"So, where do we go from here? The D.A.?"

"I guess." Bob wiped his mouth with a napkin. "That's what he's there for. I'll have to be present when they confront Harry, but it's the D.A.s case now, not mine. It makes me wonder why someone like him would throw away a twenty-year career to have sex with a kid," Bob said as Chase looked at him.

"They start out by reading porn. Then they eventually graduate when reading and looking at pictures doesn't do it anymore." He took a sip of Pepsi. "They start reading things other than soft-porn and going to places they should not be. Then they wake up one day realizing they are wrapped up in it all the way to their noses."

"Sort of like you and the bottle a few years back."

"That was a dark time."

Chapter 59

Chase sat on a lawn chair watching Matthew who was curled up in his lap asleep. Marti, Grace and Dianna had gone shopping with Janice for her upcoming wedding. Walt and Janice had finally gotten around to setting a date, and that was an opened invitation to max out her credit cards. The cattle were lowing and the ranch was peaceful, except the sound of the television inside the family room where Walt was watching the Dodgers play the Cincinnati Reds. Chase thought about tucking the boy into the playpen and watching the game with Walt, but then he could also keep holding him on his lap and watch him sleep.

He had no idea when it happened, but he couldn't picture life on the ranch without Matthew Peterson. Somehow the little squirt had wormed his way inside Chase's heart and never let go. It had somehow turned out to be the same for Marti. It was hard for him to picture life without her. She had come to him asking for help to find her daughter but never really left after they found Grace. She did have a house and a car of her own, but life seemed empty when she was gone. He knew logically that someday they would be gone. Grace would get remarried, whether it would be to Kirk Randell or someone else, and take her son away. The same could be said for Marti. She was still fairly young and beautiful. She wouldn't be single very long once the word got out.

He eased a handkerchief from his back pocket and wiped his nose. He had no idea where that left Chase McGraw. He stopped to chastise himself for feeling sorry for himself instead of being happy things were turning out so well. The one thing he couldn't understand was how he entered this case being a bachelor without any children, but wound-up having a fifteen-year-old daughter.

He watched as Janice's truck pulled through the gate and rolled to a stop next to his truck. The women climbed out chattering like a bunch of jaybirds and carried several bags to the house. Grace came back out to where he was, smiling.

"I'm sorry we're late. That took longer than we thought. I hope he wasn't too much trouble."

"Matt? No, he wasn't any trouble at all."

She carefully took her son from his arms, causing him to wiggle.

"We ate dinner and came outside to play with Buster." Chase followed as she took him inside. "Then when they got tired, Buster got a drink and curled up on the patio and Matt fell asleep in my lap."

She placed Matthew into the playpen and smiled. "Wait until you see Janice's wedding dress. I just love it."

The moment was gone. Chase smiled and complimented the women on their purchases. Janice's *wedding dress* happened to be a stark-white Rodeo Princess outfit with boot-cut legs, sequins and a white cowgirl hat. Chase had to admit the outfit made Janice look years younger, and prettier than he'd ever seen his sister. Then they were gone. Chase sat on the back patio nursing a cup of coffee, watching for the moon to slowly rise in the distance.

Okay, God. It always winds up with me coming to you, asking what you want me to do. Well, here I am again. You know how I feel. Please tell me what to do.

Chapter 60

Dianna had found a spot on the family room sofa and made herself comfortable. It had been a pretty quiet three days compared to the previous week when they had the arraignment for Kyle and Cody and their friend. They were going to be facing multiple counts of kidnapping, false imprisonment and sex-trafficking. Now Chase had a few days off while the Sheriff's Department worked with the District Attorney building an even stronger case. Janice had gone to a ladies' Bible study, and Chase was on the telephone inside the office talking to a customer, so she should not be disturbed. She opened an autographed copy of *The Doña* to where she had left off last night and began reading. She got to the part where Don Rudolfo was confronting one of the men who had molested his wife when Chase called to her.

"Hey, Dianna, get your boots on. I'm going to need your help."

"Uh, I'm never going to finish this book." She placed the bookmark between the pages and snapped the book closed.

"What are you reading?"

"This." Dianna held the book high before laying it on the coffee table.

"Oh, you'll like that one." Chase said as she slipped her boots on.

"Not if I don't read it.'"

"Well, I do need two good arms for this job, but I'll try getting you home quickly."

"What's the job?"

"Well," Chase said as they walked toward his truck, "a young girl 'borrowed' her grandmother's diamond necklace without asking and wore it to the prom then misplaced it somewhere."

"Ouch! What's it worth?" Dianna said with a chuckle.

"The insurance company has it valued at seventy-five thousand."

"Oh no. Dianna burst out laughing. "So, where do we start?"

"With her boyfriend's car."

******

"You're wasting your time." The teenage boy stood beside his parents as Chase and Dianna poked around the cream-colored Nissan. "I've checked every square inch of that car. The necklace isn't in there."

"Good, that should make our job that much easier." He looked up at Dianna.

"Did you find anything?"

"No. Did you find anything?"

"Nothing." Chase flipped the latch on the driver's seat and let the back lean against the stirring wheel then climbed into the rear seat.

"The necklace isn't in that car, I tell you. I don't know where it is." The boy repeated himself loudly.

"Dianna," Chase said with a chuckle. "Flip the driver's seat back like someone's seated there. Then, I want you to rumple around in the seats while I watch here in the back."

"Like this?" She bounced up and down and pushed with her hands against the leather.

"Yeah, just like that. Keep it going."

Dianna bounced until she was getting tired and ready to quit when Case yelled.

"Whoa, do that again."

"What? This?" Dianna said and bounced a few times.

"No, the thing you did after that. A little more to the right. Right there! Hold it!"

Chase slipped his right hand between the driver and passenger's seats and down to the metal frame. He fumbled around a little.

"Almost. Alright…got it."

"The necklace?" Dianna leaned over the back of the seat.

"No, but I found this." He handed her a pair of girl's underwear. "Could you please hand this to our young friend?"

Dianna burst out laughing and tossed the panties to the boy, who received a slap to the head by his mother.

"Okay, once more," Chase said as he fished his hand back between the seats. A minute later, Chase slowly pulled a shiny diamond necklace up into the sunlight.

"Oh, wow!" Dianna said and held it against her own neck. "This is too pretty to wear to the prom. "It really is."

The boy received another whack from his mother. "You said you checked the car."

"I did check. Every inch."

"Not very well," his father growled, "or else this man and his daughter wouldn't have found it there, would they? You're grounded until you're a hundred and ten!"

Chase thanked the parents and slipped the necklace into an envelope before starting his truck. He shook his head and laughed as they pulled into the city street.

"That's a good lesson for you…for everyone, actually. Jesus said that there's nothing done in secret that wouldn't be shouted from the housetop."

"Well, this certainly will," Dianna said. "Especially the panties. That girl's gonna have a hard time when the word gets out…and it will. Believe me, it will."

Chapter 61

Dianna Rigsby came from the house carrying two mugs of steaming coffee and gave one to Grace who was watching Chase lead Easy around the small paddock carrying Martha, who was holding Matthew.

"Careful, it's boiling hot."

"Thanks," Grace said with a warm smile.

They watched in silence for a couple of minutes, sipping coffee.

"You do realize, don't you, that you'll never be able to move very far away from Chase McGraw. He's totally in love with that baby," Dianna said.

"Mmm, yeah, the thought has crossed my mind," Grace said with a nod of her head. "Mom's going to be the same way, but I suppose there could be worse things."

Dianna sipped her coffee then laughed as she sat on a bale of straw. "I honestly don't think those two are going to move very far away from each other, let alone moving away from Matthew."

"You could be right." Grace squeezed onto the bale beside her. "I think it's kind of cute, like watching a couple of teens flirt with each other." She glanced at Dianna and grinned. "Sorry."

"No need to apologize on my account. I'm sort of like a *hurry up and get things done* girl." She moved her right arm in a straight line away from her. "If it's something that's good for you and if you really want it, then go for it. If not, why waste your time."

Grace studied her for a minute. "That's refreshing to know. I thought you were kind of different from the other girls."

They watched as Matthew giggled and waved at them when they passed.

"Can I ask you something?"

"Sure," Grace said, "fire away."

"Weren't you ever afraid being locked inside that… hell-hole?"

"Oh, every day." Grace chuckled. "Why'd you ask that?"

"You didn't act like it."

"I was petrified," Grace said. "I thought I was going to lose my mind, being locked inside a room with no windows and nowhere to go and no one to really talk with. It did teach me a lot about prayer and trusting God to get us out of there alive."

"Huh, you didn't act like it. Watching you made me want to be just like you," Dianna said and set her cup on the bale of straw.

"Thank you," Grace said giving Dianna a quick squeeze. "But all my courage came from God. I was on the verge of giving up several times, but God always seemed to give me just enough to keep me going every day. On the other hand, there were several times I admired *you*."

"Really? When?"

"Well, one time was when you sent Kyle flying down the stairs."

"Yeah," Dianna said with a laugh. "That must've been one of those God things, 'cause I was scared to death myself. I was hoping it would've broken his stupid neck."

"Nah, this way's better," Grace said, patting her on the leg. "He'll wake up every day for several years inside a prison, knowing a fifteen-year-old girl put him there."

They sat in silence for a few minutes before Dianna spoke with a quivery voice. "I get nightmares about that place and those men."

"Me too."

"Really?" How do you get them to stop?"

"I pray a lot. I pray that God will make them stop. I "also pray for you and the rest of the girls. The nightmares haven't completely stopped yet, but I'm able to live with them."

Grace set her mug next to Dianna's and took her hands.

"I've never asked, but do you know Jesus as your savior?"

"I don't know." Dianna slowly shook her head.

"We can change that right now, if you want."

"How?

"Well," Grace said quietly, "in the Bible, Romans, chapter three, verse twenty-three says everyone's a sinner. You, me…Chase and my mom and Janice…all of us have done something wrong in our lives. And Romans 6:23 says that the wages (what we earn) for our sins is death, eternal separation from God."

"Like us getting locked in the shelter."

"Exactly. But in that same verse, it says God's gift to us is eternal life in Jesus. John chapter one, verse twelve says 'as many people who receive Him, He gives the right to become the children of God. Just as many as who believes in Him.'"

"All I've got to do is believe? What about all the bad stuff I've done? I ain't no saint." Dianna looked away and shook her head.

"First John, chapter one, verse nine says, if we confess our sins to God, and tell Him all about the stuff we've done, He's faithful and righteous to forgive our sins and make us clean."

"How?" A tear mapped its way down her right cheek. "How do I do that?"

"It's kind of easy, and that's what makes some people stumble. In Revelation chapter three, verse twenty says Jesus is standing at the door to your heart, wanting to come in, Dianna. He wants to give you a new life and take away all the bad stuff. Would you like to pray now and ask Jesus to be your God and savior?"

Dianna nodded her head silently, so Grace bowed her head and led her in prayer.

******

Chase happened to glance toward Grace and Dianna and stopped the horse. He laid his hand on Martha's leg and squeezed gently.

"See that?"

"Yes, I do. What do you think is happening?"

"Well," he started the horse forward, "I'd say Grace has found her calling and I'm getting a brand new daughter."

Chapter 62

Chase bounded up the steps to Bob Thornton's office and stopped to hold the door open for a female patrol officer. The poor girl was trying to navigate the doorway with an armful of paperwork and not having much luck. He'd gotten a message on his phone from Sarah that she had some information concerning Dianna Rigsby and needed to see him as soon as possible. He entered her office with a feeling of disgust welling inside his chest. The Child Protection Services was overwhelmed with paperwork and regulations and limped along at a snail's pace, making anything good hard to find. He opened Sarah's office door and stepped inside. The woman was on the telephone and waved a sealed envelope at him. He took it and sat in one of the empty chairs. Sarah motioned for him to open the envelope as Chase just sat there.

"Open the danged envelope," she said as she hung up.

"Oh, that was what that last finger movement meant?"

"Don't be a smarty-pants and open the envelope."

"What is it, a wanted poster on Dianna?" Chase tore the end off and withdrew a small stack of papers. He looked at Sarah but her phone rang again, so Chase began thumbing through the stack, page by page. The paperwork basically said Dianna Rigsby was a true orphan as she had been claiming. She was also fifteen years old as she claimed and had above average intelligence. The only bad information came from a court-appointed psychiatrist who said she had trouble adjusting to the last home she was placed in and ran away.

"So, what do you think?" Sarah said as she hung up the phone.

"Mainly, that she's been telling the truth. She's a fifteen-year-old that looks like she's eleven or twelve." Chase cocked his head to one side and grinned. "So, what's the bottom line? Where does that leave us?"

"Look at the last two pages." Sarah got out of her chair and leaned over his shoulder. "There," she said and pointed. The last pages were written by Judge Evans stating that since Dianna was fifteen, a foster child and a key witness in a human-trafficking case, it was the court's opinion that she should be placed in the custody of Chase McGraw and live on the ranch. She was free to attend any school she chose, providing she made herself available to testify during the trial. He also said she was a part-time intern at the Sheriff's Department and came with a high recommendation.

"Really?" Chase said with a chuckle. "I remember her piddling around here in your office a few days, but I don't remember either you or Bob giving her a title."

"Well I gave it to her, and if anyone asks, I'll tell them she worked as my clerk. I would have paid her if they'd have let me. Do you have a problem with that?"

"No, not one bit." Chase held the papers shoulder high. "Your idea or Bob's?"

"Both of us. So, Chase McGraw, she's your daughter legally for now. How does that make you feel, *Daddy*?"

Chase got from his chair and hugged her tightly. "I think you guys just made a little girl very happy."

******

Dianna came in from mucking the stalls, hot and sweaty. Janice glanced at her from the stove where she was cooking dinner. "Did you finish?"

"Yes, I got it all piled up ready to do whatever you do with it."

"Good, that's tomorrow's lesson. Right now, you probably should jump in the shower. Dinner will be ready in about 45 minutes, and you smell like you've been mucking stalls."

*****

Dianna stood in the middle of the shower letting the hot water run over her tired muscles. She vaguely heard Chase laughing about something, followed by Janice and Walt's voices. She quickly shampooed her shoulder-length hair and turned several times as she rinsed off. She came from the bathroom carrying her dirty clothes balled up together.

"Oh, there you are," Janice said as she set a platter filled with pot roast on the table. "I was about ready to come and tell you dinner's ready. You can toss those beside the washer for right now."

Dianna put the dirty clothes on top of the washer and paused at her chair as she stared at the envelope leaning against her plate.

"What's this?" she said as she sat down.

"Open the envelope," Chase said with a grin.

"Okay, but what is it?"

"Read the last page. It explains it all." Chase reached to place a slice of roast on his plate.

Dianna slowly read the last page then read it again. "Does this mean what I think it says?"

"What it means is, you're my kid legally...sort of. I have custody over you and you're my responsibility, and you're supposed to mind me. We'll wait a few months then petition the court to let me adopt you. If it's alright with you of course."

Dianna got up from her chair slowly and hugged Chase from behind. "Yes it's alright with me. This has been the happiest time of my life."

"Good, Chase said with a chuckle. "Sarah Benton went to a lot of work to put this together, and she might break a chair over both our heads if we don't make this work."

Chapter 62

The court hearings for all three men went smoothly and quickly. The prosecuting attorney was a young female the District Attorney had just hired only a few months earlier and Chase worried if she was going to be up to the task. But the woman attacked like a bulldog protecting a bone, laying out a mountain of evidence beside each charge the men were facing. In the end, they were going to trial separately, with Judge Evans presiding over all three. The first trial date was set for Kyle Bolts, four months away.

******

The first two weeks of October were busy as they made the ranch winter-tight, installing storm windows and having several cords of firewood delivered and stacked inside one of the barns. Chase also gave Dianna riding lessons and lessons on the proper care of a horse. The crowning moment came when Chase hooked an empty horse trailer onto his truck and loaded Janice and Dianna into the cab with Walt. They arrived at a horse auction where Chase bought Dianna a palomino named Crackers. Dianna had begun to think she'd died and gone to heaven until Janice returned from town with several text books and paperwork.

"The school says it's only a matter of weeks until the semester is finished. They say you need to start studying at home so you won't be too far behind when you start school. We start tomorrow," she said with a grin and headed down the hall. Dianna eyed the stack of books." You've got to be kidding," she said with a loud voice. "I don't know where to start."

"That's what I'm here for," Janice said from her bedroom.

Chapter 63

"So, how is she doing?" Grace stirred her cup of hot tea.

"Oh, not too bad," Janice said with a chuckle. "She's doing better than I thought but I'm not much of a teacher; it's hard to get a straight story out of her sometimes." She passed a plate of cookies around the table. Janice had invited several women to a home Bible study. They were seated in her office enjoying coffee, tea and hot chocolate while Matthew napped inside the play pen.

"Well, I'm sure the vague answers and being private have a lot to do with what she's been through. You can ask my mom the next time you see her and she'll say the same things about me." Grace smiled and toasted Janice with her teacup.

"By the way, how is your mother," a chunky woman with a bad permanent asked.

"She is doing fine. She really wanted to be here today, but had to go to work."

"Grrr!" The sound of fists beating the table in frustration came from the kitchen where Dianna was supposed to be studying.

"Excuse me." Janice started to rise but Grace patted her on the arm.

"Let me take care of her. After all, I'm supposed to be the teacher. I guess I should find out if I can really teach."

Several of the women laughed as she left the room. Janice sat back down without saying a word and smiled.

*****

"Hi."

Dianna glanced at Grace then tossed a history book across the table. "I'm never going to understand what she wants. Her questions don't even make sense. *"*

"Ahhh," Grace said slowly and nodded her head. "I've had a couple of teachers like that myself. Let me see her notes." Grace scanned the page and chuckled.

"I can see what you're talking about. She's not very clear, is she?"

"No, she's not. I was beginning to think I'm stupid or something."

"I don't think it's you. Do you want me to help you?"

"Does the word *duh* mean anything to you?"

"Okay, here's what we're going to do. I don't want you to pay any attention to her instruction sheet. I'll rewrite it so you can understand what she wants. But first, go get a cup of tea from Janice, then come sit beside me."

By the time the Bible study hand ended, Grace had come to the conclusion that her first student was highly intelligent and knowledgeable but woefully ignorant about some things.

When Dianna left the room Grace sat there thinking. The poor girl had been bounced around from home to home and missed a lot of classroom instruction. But she seemed to learn things quickly. She should be ready to return to school by the time the next semester started.

******

Winter arrived in the middle of December by dumping heavy rain for a solid week, and three inches of snow in Tehachapi. Janice called all her part-time cowboys but two were out of the state on vacation and the other was helping tend cattle on another ranch. Chase placed his private investigations company on hold and worked beside Walt and Janice, checking on the cattle and hauling hay. On the first day, they returned home as the sun turned into an orange ball of fire and sank lower in the western sky. Janice opened the door to be assaulted with the aroma of beef stew and homemade bread.

"All of you go climb into the shower. You're coated with mud," Dianna said. "Just toss your clothes into the hallway and I'll take care of them." The following day, she met them at the barn at sunrise and tossed a saddle on Crackers.

"And where do you think you're going?" Chase pulled on the leather cinches on his saddle.

"To help the cattle, same as you."

"And what about school?" Janice asked.

"What about it?" Dianna tightened her own cinches. "I'm caught up with the rest of the class. Go ahead and call my teacher. She'll tell you the truth. Besides, it won't kill me to miss a couple of days of school."

"I hate to butt in," Walt said, "but I say let her come. She'll be a help to us and the cattle both. If not, you can expect the toll of sick and dying cattle to rise."

"Okay," Janice said as she led Easy toward the barn door. "I guess I'd better see about something for lunch and dinner."

"It's already been taken care of." Dianna swung into the saddle. "I called Grace last night and she and her mother will meet us at the old picnic table by the creek at noon."

"They can't go down that road in her car. It's nothing but mud. You'd better call them and tell them not to come." Chase placed one hand on his hip.

"Who said anything about Marti's car? I left the keys to your truck on the counter, and, the coffee should be about finished. I set a couple of thermoses by the pot. Now, are we going to go take care of cattle, or just argue about me wanting to help?"

"My truck?" A deep crease appeared between Chase's eyes.

"You can wash the crud off you're truck a lot easier than raise a cow from the dead," Walt said with a snicker. "Come on, girl," he said to Dianna. "You can be my saddle-pard for the day. Those two will argue all day."

Dianna snuck a glance toward Chase and caught him grinning at her and she smiled back. Chase and Walt hooked a large horse trailer to Janice's three-quarter ton truck. Dianna propped the doors open and they loaded a dozen bales of hay into the trailer then put the horses inside. Chase kicked the truck into 4-wheel drive and swung the trailer around, following a trail across the rolling hills. They hadn't covered a quarter of a mile before they stopped the truck and rescued three calves stuck in mud. That seemed to set the pace for the remaining day. By the time Janice parked her truck that evening, it was all Dianna could do to keep her eyes open.

"Here, girl. I'll take care of your hoss. You did good today." Walt gave her a gentle swat on the back and took Cracker's reins.

"You sure?"

"Sure I'm sure. Get in the shower before those two use all the hot water."

"I think I will." She gave him a quick hug and headed toward the house. The smell of bacon and fresh baked biscuits assaulted her nose before she reached the porch. Grace held the door open and roared with laughter.

"What in the world happened to you?"

"The worst thing was I got pulled off Crackers by a brindle calf and drug through a puddle of mud." She glanced toward Matthew who clung to his grandma Marti's leg.

"Yeah, I guess I should go clean up."

******

215

They were joined by Grace the following day. It only took a couple of hours before a mother cow mistook Grace dropping a lasso on her calf as an act of aggression and charged. Her horse bolted toward higher ground, leaving Grace lying face-down in the mud.

"Ya! Get outta here," Chase yelled and swatted at the mother with his coiled rope. "You okay?" he asked as he leaned in the saddle and offered her a hand. Grace took the hand and struggled to her feet. That's when Chase started laughing.

"What? What are you laughing at?" Grace quickly checked herself.

"You ... I'm laughing at you. There isn't a clean spot on you, from head to foot."

Chase pulled the calf from the mire, then retrieved her horse.

"Don't let it bother you. It's happened to us all one time or other." He handed her the reins.

"Thank you. I appreciate your help."

"You're welcome." Grace waited until he turned away.

"Oh, Chase?"

"Yes?" He looked back at her and got hit with a glob of mud. "Hey!" he yelled.

Grace walked her horse next to his and grinned.

"Don't let it bother you, Mr. McGraw. You were too clean."

"You little devil." He grabbed for her but she leaned away with a giggle.

"You'd better be nice, or I'll tell my mother on you."

******

Grace and Dianna tied their horses to one of the fence rails and got ready to close the gates when Chase, Walt and Janice drove the last of the cattle into the upper pasture. It was mid-afternoon on Thursday, and they were finished with the rescue.

"Yah, get back in there," Chase yelled as he swatted at young bull who tried to make an escape. Dianna and Grace swung their gate closed and Janice latched them shut.

"Well, I hope that's the last time we have to do that for a while."

"Me too," Walt said. "But take a look at that bunch of young cows you've got locked inside that paddock. I think that's the largest crop of cows I've seen in a while."

"Yeah, I agree," Janice said. "But I still don't want to repeat this past week. Do you?"

Dianna helped care for the horses and fed the chickens before showering. She drew a few stares when she showed up at the dinner table in her pajamas.

"Well, look at you. Are you out of clean clothes?" Janice said.

"No, but right after we eat, I'm going to bed and don't expect me to wake until I've slept most of tomorrow."

"Huh," Chase said thoughtfully. "That's too bad."

"How's that?"

"They're opening this year's Stampede tomorrow with a dance and barbeque. I've already reserved tickets for everyone, but if you're going to sleep all day, I guess I can give your ticket to someone else."

"Yeah, and I was hoping to introduce you to my nephew," Walt said as he spooned some fried potatoes onto his plate.

"Ray's going to be here?" Janice said.

"That's what he says. He'll be here around noon tomorrow."

"Oh," Janice nodded. "I guess he'll get to see Dianna in her P.J.s."

"What do I care if some old coot sees me like this? I'm tired. And if you're done with the potatoes, pass 'em this way."

Walt grinned as he passed the bowl of potatoes. "Ray's nineteen and hails from Amarillo. He was a junior roping champion, and he's decided to turn pro this year. I thought you might want to see a fellow Texan."

"We're leaving around one tomorrow afternoon, so be ready if you want to go." Chase grinned as he passed her a plate of biscuits.

Chapter 64

Dianna stared at the young hunk standing in front of her. "My name's Ray Evers."

The top of her head might reach the middle of his chest, hat and all. It took a few seconds for her to recover before she shook his hand. "Hi, I'm Dianna Rigsby."

"I don't know about you, but I'm starving, We'd better get in line before it gets any longer."

Dianna followed him through the line and returned to the picnic table with her plate piled high with barbequed ribs, garlic bread and ranch beans. Ray squeezed in beside her. Their family and friends took up the entire table, making conversation easy, although Dianna chose to say very little and only spoke when someone asked her a question. Ray took her empty plate to the trash can and returned as a local country and western band took the stage.

"Know how to Texas line dance?"

Dianna stared up as Ray offered his hand.

"Are you kidding? My grandparents owned a small ranch outside Austin. What do you think?" Dianna grabbed his hand as she slid away from the table.

"Well, I guess I don't need to worry about her the rest of the day," Chase said with a laugh. "Come on, let's teach them how to dance." He held out his hand to Marti.

"Uh, I'm not very good, Chase."

"Who cares. It's all in fun." He grabbed her hand and led to grassy area in front of the band where he led her in a Texas two-step. He held onto Marti as the band switched songs and they kept dancing. It was getting close to nine o'clock when Grace motioned for them to stop.

"I'm sorry to break up a perfectly good dance, but I should take Matthew home. It's past his bedtime."

"I can bring Dianna home, Mr. McGraw," Ray said as Chase broke up a lively line dance. "I'll take care of her...I promise."

Chase glanced toward Dianna who was now silently begging. "Okay, but keep her on a short leash. I'm counting on you."

They didn't see much of Dianna for the next two days as she became Ray's shadow during the rodeo. He placed second in team roping then he and Walt put on an exhibition that went, in Walt's words, "smooth as frog hair."

Janice and Walt were married on Monday evening in a small wedding on their back patio, with Ray as Walt's best man. They were going to leave for a week-long honeymoon in Monterey the following day. It was eight o'clock Tuesday morning and Ray was sitting behind the wheel of his Chevy truck at Janice's ranch, preparing to leave for Prescott, Arizona. Dianna leaped up on the running board and planted a passionate kiss on his lips.

"That's just so you know how I feel, Raymond Evers." He grabbed her behind the head and returned the kiss, then left without another word. Dianna spent the remainder of the day floating on a cloud.

Chapter 65

Dianna gripped Chase's hand in a death grip as she tapped her foot. The three men were ushered into the courtroom and seated up front. He glanced toward Marti and Grace. Both women were seated silently and gave the appearance of calm assurance that everything was going to be okay. The bailiff rapped the gavel as the door behind the large podium opened.

"Hear ye, hear ye. All stand. The honorable Judge Robert Evans presiding." Everyone inside the crowded courtroom stood then sat as he was seated. The first day of the hearing went pretty much as Chase expected. The charges were read and the defendants pled innocent, meaning a jury would be picked. Chase was disappointed, in that Grace had been making regular visits to the jail to see Cody, and he was interested to see if the visits made any difference.

It was near the end of the second day of the hearing that things seemed to explode. Kyle Bolts was in the middle of blaming Cody as the mastermind of the entire operation and Cody jumped to his feet. Judge Evans had to call for extra bailiffs to restore order. Kyle evidently thought it would be cute to flash an obscene gesture toward Cody, which caused Judge Evans to call a halt to the proceedings until further notice.

******

"I thought for a second that Kyle might hurt someone," Grace said. Chase had led them all to his favorite restaurant, the street cart by the courthouse.

"Why?" Bob Thornton glanced at Grace while he applied mustard to his Polish sandwich.

"Why? He's so big and strong…"

"Nah, he lets off a lot of hot air." Bob laughed. "My goodness," he pointed his sandwich at Dianna, "she beat the stuffings out of him. What do you weigh, honey, a hundred pounds?"

"One hundred and seven, last time I checked."

"See that's what I'm talking about." Bob took a large bite and chewed.

"He is pretty big, Bob," Marti said.

"Yeah, he is that. And if you stood still long enough, he might knock you down. But if they ever got into it again, I'm placing my money on Di."

"So, what happens next," Grace asked softly.

"We'll have three separate trials. that could take most of the year, maybe longer, before it's done. We'll all be called to testify. My only fear is they'll come to some plea bargain and they'll get off easy."

"Maybe not," Chase set a bag on the bench beside Bob. "Cody's fit to be tied being blamed for everything. He just might talk."

"I hope you're right," Bob said. He cocked his head toward Grace. "Think you're up for another Cody visit?"

"I think so."

******

Cody was still angry and vented to Grace like an opened fire hydrant. Grace suggested he repeat what he was saying to a recorder and he agreed. Bob passed the recording to Judge Evans, who reconvened the hearing, but they only called for Cody Waters. The trial went quickly with the prosecutor attacking with a vengeance. All three men were found guilty. Now, it was simply a matter of sentencing.

Chapter 66

Chase stood inside the kitchen drinking a cup of coffee and staring out the window. Janice and Walt were on their honeymoon, leaving Chase in charge of both the ranch and McGraw Investigations. Dianna came from her bedroom and hugged him from behind. He placed his hands over hers before kissing her knuckles.

"You through talking to Ray?"

"Yeah."

"Where is he now?" He led her to the sofa and sat beside her, still holding her hand.

"Oakdale, up north."

"Really? That's only three to four hours away. Maybe if Janice and Walt get back in time, you and I can take off and visit him."

"Oh, that would be great, Pops. But what about you? Don't you have a couple of cases you're working on?"

"Nothing that can't wait."

They sat silently for a few minutes. Dianna tucked her feet under herself and studied him closely.

"What?" Chase studied her back.

"You miss them, don't you?"

"Miss who?"

"Come on, Pops. Marti and Grace."

"Mmm, yeah, but don't forget Matthew. I miss seeing him too."

"Okay, I can't forget Matthew. We haven't seen them in over two weeks now. Give them a call."

"I will...maybe in another week or so. They need some time for themselves."

"I thought you were the one who didn't believe in letting things go. Whatever happened to that man?"

"He's still around, but there's some stuff you don't understand."

"Like what?"

Chase turned away to watch the cattle through the window, milling in the pen next to the barn. "Stuff." Dianna finally gave up and returned to her bedroom and the autographed photograph she'd received from Ray. Maybe Janice knew what to do. She'd ask her when they got home.

Chapter 67

Chase was walking his horse through a small herd of cattle that had been corralled near the house, aimlessly doing nothing. Janice came from the kitchen carrying two cups of coffee and handed one of them to Dianna who was perched on a bale of hay and chewing on a straw.

"What's he up to?" Janice took a sip from her cup.

"Heck if I know. He's been like that for hours."

"Yeah, it sort of hits men like that sometimes," Janice said with a chuckle.

"What does?"

"Love. Don't you recognize it?"

"Not if it makes you crazy. I think I love Ray, but nothing like that. He's gone nuts! He doesn't eat enough to keep a sparrow alive, and he won't work. He's just crazy." She sipped her coffee.

"Well, it's coming for you too, honey, so prepare yourself. Here, hold this for me." Janice handed her coffee cup to Dianna and entered the paddock. She wove her way through the small herd until she reached Chase and grabbed the horse's halter.

"You might as well go see her."

"See who?"

"See Marti, you numbskull."

"Why do I need to see her? I found Grace, and that's what she hired me for."

"Well, first of all," Janice took a step back to glare at her brother. "You didn't find Grace, God did that. We were getting nowhere fast until we all started praying then God took over."

"Well, yeah, you're right. God did find her," Chase said. "But..."

"But nothing. You've been moping around here for over a week now like a lost puppy dog. Now, give her a call and go tell her how you feel."

Chase stared at her with a blank look on his face.

"I mean it, Chase McGraw. If you don't straighten up, I'm going to have Walt and Dianna hold you down so I can apply the tickle method." Janice grinned at him.

"You wouldn't dare."

"Try me."

"Okay, I'll go see her. What should I say?"

"Do you love her?"

Chase looked off into the distance. "I didn't think so at first but, yes I think I do."

"Then tell her that, you big dummy. I want the both of you acting somewhat normal by the time my wedding rolls around in a few weeks."

******

Chase watched Janice retreat inside the house before dismounting and pulling his cell phone from this pocket. He didn't have to search for Marti's number. It was programmed into the phone and highlighted. He punched the number and placed the phone next to his ear.

"Hello, Chase. I was wondering when you might call. How are you?"

The sound of her voice made him feel like being covered with a warm blanket on a cold winter day.

"Oh, I've been doing fine. How about yourself?"

"I've been good."

"How about Matthew?"

"Matthew's good, but I think he misses you. He was asking about you this morning."

"Yeah, I miss him too."

"Is there a particular reason you called, Chase? Grace and I were about to leave. We're going to take Matthew to see the new Disney movie."

"Oh? Well, actually there was. If it is alright, I'd like to have lunch with you guys tomorrow. My treat. I'll bring it to your house. That is, if it's agreeable, of course."

"Sure. It would be nice to see you again. Around twelve o'clock noon?"

"Sure; see you at twelve."

Chase hung up the telephone as a strange feeling almost like jealousy swept over him. But he had nothing to be jealous about. It was natural for a grandmother to take her grandson to see a movie. But to be honest, he wanted to sit beside Marti Black and hold her hand, put his arm around her shoulders, maybe kiss her lips.

"Ah, you're an idiot, Chase McGraw. A real idiot."

******

Chase parked his truck in front of Marti's home and turned off the engine. He glanced at Dianna, who had insisted on tagging along.

"Ready, Pops?" She gave him a toothy grin.

"Not really, but I'll be double sorry if I don't."

"That's what I thought." She patted his leg and opened the door before collecting several McDonald's paper bags. She stopped to stare at him. "Well, come on. This won't work without you."

Chase climbed out of the driver's seat and helped Buster from the back seat of the truck. It had only been one and a half weeks, but felt like an eternity. Things were changing at lightning speed and he felt like he'd been left behind with a flat tire. He followed Dianna down the sidewalk toward the front door. Even she had changed somewhat. When he first saw her, she was wearing dirty jeans with holes everywhere and ragged tennis shoes.

Today, after her shopping trip, she was wearing new jeans and cowgirl boots and sporting a straw cowgirl hat. If he didn't know her he would think she was a local girl bred and raised on a ranch.

Dianna rang the doorbell and stepped back as the door opened. Grace smiled at her and stepped back.

"Come in." She glanced at the McDonald bags and laughed. "This is lunch?"

"What did he bring?" Marti's voice floated toward them from the living room floor where she was finishing changing Matthew's diaper.

"McDonalds," Grace said over her shoulder.

"Oh, I should have warned you. He's a junk-food junkie."

Matthew stood up as Buster dashed inside. The dog sent Matthew sprawling on the carpet as he barked and licked him in the face.

"I take it they missed each other." Dianna said as Matthew wrapped his legs around Buster's waist then he and the dog wrestled over a dog toy.

"What's not to miss? Chase said.

"Well, I can see we're going to have to make some dietary changes, Mr. McGraw." Marti said.

"Why, what's wrong with it?"

"Your sister told me the hospital said your arteries are almost packed solid," she said with a snort. "Keep it up and you'll keel over with a stroke or heart attack."

Dianna held up two Happy Meals. "I take it these are for Matthew?"

"One of them is," Chase said. "The other one is Buster's."

"You bought your dog a Happy Meal?" Marti laughed out loud. "Are you trying to kill him too?"

"No, but once in a while is okay, isn't it? Besides, he earned it."

Matthew finally broke free from his wrestling match with Buster and came to see Chase's arm. He gently touched the scar left by Cody's wrench and leaned to kiss it.

"Ah, that's cute. He kissed your owie," Dianna said.

"Well, let's eat. Then maybe we'll find out why Chase came to see us," Marti said.

It took Buster almost twelve seconds to finish his Happy Meal then he started begging for hand-outs from Matthew. Grace put him in the back yard at Chase's urging.

"I received your bill," Marti said, staring at Chase.

"And?"

"And I'm sure you spent more than two hundred dollars, Mr. McGraw."

"Well, maybe, but I've been reimbursed well."

"How so?"

"An insurance company hired me to locate a missing diamond necklace." He shrugged. "I wanted to charge them by the hour, but the thing is worth more than a truck full of money. They insisted I take a percentage. So I agreed. It took Dianna and me maybe a half an hour to find it, and we made a small fortune."

Chase popped a french fry into his mouth and grinned. "You're bill has been paid. The two hundred is a token charge just to say the case is closed."

"Well, thank you."

"You're welcome."

"Oh, before I forget. Grace and Kirk are going to get married."

"Really? Congratulations. When did this happen?"

"He came over last night and asked me," Grace said with a soft smile. "I said yes. We're both going to work with children who have been abducted and sold through human trafficking."

"Wow! That's a big change, but it's needed. I hope I'm invited to the wedding."

"Certainly; you, Janice, Dianna and Walt of course. You're all invited to the wedding. You should get the invitations in a day or two. In fact, I would like Dianna to be one of my bride's maids."

"Oh, thank you," Dianna said. "What am I supposed to wear? I've never been one before."

"We'll work all that out ahead of time," Marti said.

They sat silently around the table for what seemed an eternity. It was Marti who finally broke the silence.

"All of this seems so unnatural."

"What does?" Grace asked.

"All this. You getting kidnapped and put in with these young girls. Then you're almost sold to someone somewhere we don't know. None of it makes much sense. I really wish someone would explain why people do things that hurt other people, and act as though none of it bothers them."

"That's because it doesn't bother them," Chase said with a shrug."

"Well, it should," Marti said passionately. I really went through hell during that time, and I can't imagine what Grace and the girls went through. She wakes up at night crying and begging to go home."

"It bothered me too, and still does. But I decided I wasn't going to get sold as a slave to any one if I could help it," Dianna said. "What about you, Pops? Did any of that bother you?"

Chase sat staring at his soft drink cup as he turned it several times on the table.

"Pops?"

"It bothers cops a lot. It's just that they see this type of stuff so often and up close that they press it down deep inside. If they didn't they'd go nuts and no one could stand to be around them. Me?" he shrugged again, "yeah, it bothered me a lot. Especially when I didn't know if I could solve the case. It was God who made the difference."

"Well, that brings me back to the question that I've been dying to get answered. Why would a loving god allow such things to happen, especially to children?" Marti sipped her Pepsi.

"Well," Chase sat upright in his chair. "what if God washed his hands of us all and let things happen as they will. None of this would have happened. Oh, the girls might have been sold, but none of us would have met each other. You and I wouldn't have met. You and Grace wouldn't have met Janice or Walt. I wouldn't have met Matthew or Dianna and six girls would have been sold as slaves and the bad guys would still be out there somewhere, getting ready to do it all over again. That's why I think God involves us in his work."

"Well," Marti said slowly, "you gave me a lot to think about, Chase McGraw. I'll really have to pray about it. But that wasn't what you came by for, was it?"

"No." Chase shook his head.

"What was it you wanted, Mr. McGraw?"

"Well, I need to tell you something."

"Yes?"

"Yes." Chase's eyes watered and his voice became soft. "I've been miserable the past two weeks. I got used to having you around, Marti. Your smell, your touch...your sound. I got used to having Matthew around to scuffle with when I got home, and I miss talking to Grace. In short, I miss you and your family, Marti Black."

"You do?" she said with a grin.

"I was hoping...I don't know...I was hoping you kind of missed having me around also."

"Oh, I do miss having you around, very much." She waited a few seconds. "Is there anything else?"

"For heaven's sake Dad, ask her," Dianna said, shaking her head.

"Is there something you wanted to ask?"

"Will you marry me?"

"Of course I'll marry you, Chase McGraw. All you had to do was ask."

End

231

Thank You

We sincerely hope you've enjoyed reading *Finding Grace*. Please visit our website for other books written by this author.

www.majormitchell.net

MAJOR MITCHELL is the author of ten historical westerns, three contemporary novels and three children's books. He lives with his wife, Judy, in Northern California. He is a member of The Western Writers of America and a frequent guest speaker at historical meetings and schools on the west coast. He has also written several songs, and takes the stage on rare occasions as a singer.

CPSIA information can be obtained
at www.ICGtesting.com
Printed in the USA
BVHW030801221022
649807BV00003B/38

9 781735 129761